The Dragon's Tapestry

Martine Bates

Red Deer College Press

Northern Lights Young Novels are published by
Red Deer College Press
56 Avenue & 32 Street Box 5005
Red Deer Alberta Canada T4N 5H5

Edited for the Press by Tim Wynne-Jones
Cover art & design by Ron Lightburn
Text design by Dennis Johnson
Printed & bound in Canada by Friesen Corp.
for Red Deer College Press

The Publishers gratefully acknowledge the financial contribution of
the Alberta Foundation for the Arts, Alberta Culture & Multicultur-
alism, The Canada Council, Red Deer College & Radio 7 CKRD

Canadian Cataloguing in Publication Data
Bates, Martine, 1953–
The dragon's tapestry
ISBN 0-88995-080-6
I. Title II. Author
PS8553.A84D7 1992 jC813'.54 C91-091823-6
PZ7.B384Dr 1992

To Larry,
who was the first to believe

"*F*aerie contains many things ... besides dwarfs, witches, trolls, giants, or dragons: it holds the seas, the sun, the moon, the sky; and the earth, and all things that are in it: tree and bird, water and stone, wine and bread, and ourselves, mortal men, when we are enchanted."

–J. R. R. Tolkien, *Tree and Leaf*

PROLOGUE

GRONDIL, THE Oldwife, felt Srill's eyes upon her, felt the young woman listening intently to every word she said. Sometimes a movement, a breath, the slightest change, and Grondil would stop and, with her hand on Srill's belly, would measure her pain, share it. The magic felt strong.

"The child's life thread is a long one," Grondil said, measuring out the first of the threads to be laid beside the inkle loom in the order that she would need them. She did not see Srill smile. The warp had already been wound around the pegs in readiness, but her hands would need to be quick in order to finish the tapestry before the child was born.

For years, since the death of her mother, Grondil had been alone, but during a birthing there would often be many hands to help and her house would be full. For Srill who had no husband,

5

however, there would be no help and no hands but Grondil's own to deliver the child and work the tapestry. It was dangerous having no witness to the tapestry. If it were lost or destroyed, it could not be remade. But Srill had seemed almost glad when she had come to Grondil, full of pain and joy, alone.

Grondil's fingers felt heavy and clumsy as she passed the shuttle through the sheds of the loom. Her head felt light, her neck muscles tense. She had known Srill a little, though the girl was younger. She was a quiet thoughtful lass, slow to speak like her father, dutiful and dogged like her mother, and lacking Grondil thought, the ability to laugh. But Grondil admired her, for when she spoke in her soft voice, never in gossip, everyone listened and often agreed. Srill was devout, always attending to the magic, and was kind to Grondil. One day a black-haired traveler had come through the village—what had his name been?—a lithe and lively poet with a voice like summer wind, and before he went away, he had left a child in Srill. Never mind what the villagers said, Grondil would do her best for Srill in the tapestry making. Every child received a tapestry at birth. Without it one had no soul. But for Srill's child Grondil would do her best work.

The tapestry was everyone's most treasured possession. Some said the symbols woven into it predicted one's destiny, others said they guided agency. But all believed that each symbol and design was to be carefully understood and followed. The tapestry was a sacred thing, each one a poem of prophecy not to be displayed, shown perhaps only to loved ones or to the Oldwife. At one's death the Oldwife would fold the tapestry and place it under the head of the corpse so that the spirit could carry it and with it find safe passage to the lands of the dead. Only two had Grondil seen unfulfilled. Remembering those two times made her shudder.

Grondil uttered a brief spell on her hands and searched her mind for a Song. At first the words came to her lips clumsily, whispered and toneless:

from thy deep wellsprings
oh, one Mother, grant me thy chalice
full with thy bounty of blood
that cleanses
and brings forth life
and life
and the leaving of life

The walls seemed to fall away, and Grondil was in an abyss of magic. She felt safe here, having been here many times and knowing that in the mind of the magic her will was not her own. The abyss was deep, but this time she went deeper than she had ever been before, deep into the ancient voids where the oldest magic boiled. Grondil went white-blind with tears in the joy of it. She stopped to let the tears dry in her eyes and to look at Srill. The young woman was still, her brow knit in concentration, her breath coming in soft pants, her lips oddly twisted. Grondil gave herself up to the tapestry making, allowing the magic to use her. No sooner had she done this than a picture began to fill her mind: the seven moons of Ve, symbolizing womanliness and beauty. The child would be a girl. She thought of the verse she had learned as a child to remember them by:

Clewdroin, Opo, Epsilon, Non;
Globa, Septa, Orbica yon.

She portrayed them as she had last seen them in winterdark: Epsilon, a great airy ball of celestial sapphire, Opo and Non like two pink eyes askew above the horizon, Orbica like a jade bowl in the star-sugared sky.

As the moons began to take shape, Grondil sang her soft

chant. She felt capable of her calling, aware of the magic that used her to fathom the being of this new baby and to speak its destiny.

After the moons came flowers, sunrise-colored humelodia and brilliant white ice gozzys. Grondil wondered for a moment why the two appeared together, the one symbolizing life and the other death. Other symbols came: a crown, a key, a rare and beautiful tree such as she heard grew in the mountains of Verduma.

Time dissolved until she felt the warmth of the estwind on her back and arms through her spidersilk.

Hours had passed.

The Song died in her throat, and Grondil realized that she was thirsty, but there would be no food or water until the tapestry was completed upon the baby's birth. As her own voice became still, she heard Srill's breath come in rageful gasps. Grondil looked at her. Rivulets of sweat on the young woman's temples ran into her hair, her eyes were unseeing and her hands were white knots of muscle. Grondil saw but only as if from a great distance. Muttering a spell of comfort, she went back to the tapestry, to the little world she was creating in color and thread.

The magic had never been so strong with her. Everywhere she looked she knew more clearly than ever before the names and beings of each object that fell into her vision. She wondered and waited for the image that would be the next part of the tapestry.

It was a mountain, a true mountain of Verduma, peaked in snow and cloud, a god's fist of bare jagged rock. Long life the mountain often symbolized, but Grondil had only seen Venutian hills woven into the tapestries.

She began to record it in detail: a tract of snow, a rock, a patch of dirt ... until it almost seemed as if she were there, the pebbles and plants beneath her feet....

Somewhere, she knew, her body still sat before the inkle loom, and her fingers, aided by spells, threaded in the image of the mountain. But Grondil was here. She was looking down into a shadowy valley, a valley that had appeared only as a streak of black on the tapestry. There was no wind, only an airless cold that breathed up from the valley. It was not dark but twilight, the stars pale. A scabbing lichen stained the raw-edged rocks at the lip of the cliff, and the smell of burning filled her nostrils.

"You come by an unknown path," she heard a voice say slowly, a voice that sounded like wind in the grass.

Grondil turned around, her back to the abyss.

"Serpent!" she whispered.

A vast scaled creature haunched before her, lean-loined and diaphanous-winged. A beautiful curl of blue fire from its mouth burned in the air a moment and was gone.

"Who are you? Why have you brought me to this place?" Grondil asked.

"It is I who should ask, 'Who are you?'" the Serpent hissed in a voice like wind in fire. "This is my prison. You are the intruder here." The creature blinked its eyes slowly. "But no, I think I know you now—you weave the tapestry of one who will be mine."

Grondil shivered in the cold windless air. Beyond the dragon she could see a wasteland of black rock thinly covered with grass. To the left was a forested area that stretched to the mountains and climbed to cloud-misted peaks. Trees. She had read about them, heard about them. There were no such trees in Venutia. But even the trees she noticed only vaguely, for the wonder of the dragon filled her vision.

The dragon spoke: "In the valley live those spirits whose tapestries are unfulfilled at the time of their deaths. I gather them like jewels to my kingdom. They are my treasure. The child and her father will be my most precious gems."

Grondil looked furtively at the creature. Her stomach felt heavy and sick, as if it were filled with a cold stone.

"The souls that come here labor on, trying to fulfill their destinies, but it must be done without hope, for I am their king, a jealous master, and I love them. This child will be the jewel in my crown and will establish my throne, for there will be no one else to withstand me. Once there were many dragons in Ve. There shall be again."

The dragon arched its sinuous neck, and a blazing breath of fire billowed into the sky. In its cold yellow eyes, Grondil sensed the weight of its evil, and she knew that her gentle powers were nothing against it.

Grondil began to run. She ran through the leafless trees, jumping over the whitened bones of broken tree limbs, weaving between bleached saplings that leaned toward the dim light like starving things. Fragments of fall's left-over season still clung to the branches and crumbled as she brushed them. A scream seemed to come from the valley. She fell, and as she fell the distant peaks became more distant until they were like the image woven on a tapestry, and it was Srill's screams that filled Grondil's ears. Her hands were again her own, though they continued to work outside her will.

"A dream, a dream," she whispered aloud to comfort herself, but before the words were spoken, she knew it was not a dream and that this deeper magic had taken her to a true place.

The tapestry before her was almost complete, as was Srill's labor. Grondil stared at the tapestry, horrified. How could she put this mountain of shadows and half-death into the life of this new child? She looked at Srill who shuddered and was still as the pain eased for a moment. She smiled feebly at Grondil.

"My baby ... will she be great and good?"

Grondil said nothing. She turned back to the tapestry and forced her hands to weave ... weave ... weave the sign of the wingwand, which was the sign of power, of magic, the sign of the Oldwife. Perhaps with this lesser magic, Grondil's own magic, the child would have some power against the dragon or better, power to fulfill her tapestry and avoid that land.

Far away she heard the dragon's laughter. She knew it would not be enough. Only the wizard's sign, the sign of the staff, was greater, and only one child could receive that sign—the wizard's child. Grondil thought of the traveler, a Verduman she thought, from his dark coloring, and she remembered the laughter in his songs. Once she had surprised herself by allowing him to take and read her book, her *Songs of the One Mother,* and when he returned it, he had drawn dragons in all the margins. In that moment she knew that the poet had indeed seen a dragon, for the drawings were true. She remembered his eyes, how beneath the laughter one day, she thought she had seen a deep sadness. All these things filled Grondil's mind, numbing her awareness of anything else while she threaded in a wingwand, a white arthropod with bloodred eyes. Then Srill called out: "The child is born! Help me."

Grondil stood on weakened legs.

"Peace, Srill," she said. Her fingers shook as she cleared the baby's mouth of mucous, tied the cord and cut it with a white-hot knife. Wrapping the child in a warm blanket, Grondil put the baby to Srill's breast. The child sucked lustily, and Srill fell asleep quickly and heavily with the child in bed beside her.

Grondil became more aware of her surroundings, above all the smell of sweat and blood. Intense fatigue made her legs tremble, and she sat down at her loom. She knew she should tie off the tapestry immediately after tying the umbilical cord, but her fingers were too weak, and at last she dozed with her head on the base of the loom.

While she slept she dreamed, and in her dream she saw the poet, the father of the babe. He was walking away toward a land of mists and twilight, and in his hand he held a staff, a wizard's staff.

A soft shuffling step at the doorway woke Grondil. She did not move. She had heard this step before: a mild crippled gait that was slow and sure. It was the Taker, the old mistress of death. Twice or three times Grondil had seen her. But this time she was too tired, and she feigned sleep, still leaning uncomfortably against the loom. She waited for the footsteps, now belonging to two, to leave her house. With a great weariness, Grondil slept again.

When the baby wailed two winds later, Grondil woke with pain in her head and neck but feeling rested. She felt no sadness as she administered to Srill not the rites of new motherhood but the rites of the dead. As she spoke the Death Song, she remembered the depth of the magic into which she had fallen while doing the child's tapestry, and she remembered the dragon's laughter and the dream of the poet carrying a staff. Gently she picked up the baby. Her cry was deep and sad. Of course it could not be, but then Grondil was astonished for she saw tears on the baby's face. Infants produced no tears. Then another tear trickled down the baby's cheek—Grondil's own.

The child's mother was dead, and with no father's house to claim the child, she would be left in the hills where surely the

Taker, with her shuffling crippled feet, would find her and gather her up into her stiff arms and take her to the babe's mother.

The infant turned her head to Grondil's breast, searching for milk. "Already you have nursed on death's milk, poor wee one," she said touching the tiny fingers. From her midwife's stores she drew, knowing she should not, a cloth dug. She soaked it in a pail of settling goat's milk and offered it to the baby who suckled noisily. Some hard place inside Grondil relented, and from that moment she loved the child and knew the child's destiny.

"Marwen you shall be called," she whispered.

She went back to her loom, placed the infant in her lap and began to weave once more.

Along the top like a border, she wove the sign of the staff. When it was done, she dug a hole in the dirt floor of her kitchen, and wrapping the baby's tapestry in oilcloth, she placed it where no one would find it.

CHAPTER ONE

AFTER MORTAL LAW THERE IS THE LAW OF THE
GODS. IT IS IN SOME WORLDS REFERRED TO
AS MAGIC. —*TENETS OF THE TAPESTRY*

MARWEN HEFTED the waterjar filled with spring water and turned to go home. This one chore she detested less than others, for she could ramble and dawdle in the hills and be alone for a time.

Marwen had always known that the hills of Marmawell were enchanted. She wondered that none of the other villagers could see it. Softly grassed, like fur, they were alive to her, pulsing with a molten heart. She knew each rise and swell, each rounded profile. Some hills were no more than fleshy mounds, shoulders and hips or cleft like breasts; some had faces that spoke to her of spellbound princes doomed to see without blinking the passing of the eons; some were moldering giants covered by a thin layer of dust, with rocks protruding in a row like spines; and some, strange nurseries with boulders nestled like great eggs in the grasses.

In the warm soft light of the dawnmonth, the dew burnished the slopes of grass and gleamed on yellow beegems. Even the insects flew past her swift and straight, their flight purposeful in the dawnspring morning. Marwen faced the wind, which blew straight and hard and low along the ground. She spread her arms and knew she was the first obstacle the wind had met for many furlongs, and so it would know it was wind again.

She could scarcely remember now the long months of winterdark. It seemed to her as if her life had begun only this day, for at last Council Grondil had kept her long promise to make Marwen her apprentice when she came of age in her sixteenth sun. Grondil was the Oldwife of Marmawell, one of those women in whose order was found the last vestiges of magic and power in all Ve. Their task as Oldwives was to weave the tapestry for each child at birth, their gift to interpret the tapestry for all who asked. In each town and village, the influence they wielded was great, for their hand was over wedding feast and mourner's fast alike.

No one in Marmawell dared murmur when Grondil announced her intentions and her adept. From the time Marwen had been a young child, she had shown a predilection for magic: a pink flower stroked into purple before the eyes of the other children, a dream come true, pictures fashioned of hearthsmoke that vanished but not before all had seen. None dared murmur, for Grondil loved her young charge, and there would be no swaying her. Many whispered among themselves that the girl was unseemly in the use of her talent, but, if the truth be known, they feared her precocity. A few grumbled that it would be bad luck, that she was not Grondil's true daughter and that she had no tapestry to validate her calling, the people of Ve being of long and lawful tradition. They said she had no tapestry at all and thus no soul—what could the magic be in the hands of a soulless one?

But it was done and Marwen rejoiced. Her hand went down to the beautiful tapestry pouch at her side. At one's apprentice-ship, one was considered old enough to carry the tapestry, and Grondil had put many hours of work into Marwen's pouch. Marwen had been so long among the villagers without a tapestry that the villagers scarcely thought it worth quarreling about when she had begun to wear the pouch with nothing to put in it, though some had glowered and gossiped.

"Someday," Grondil whispered when she had tied it to Mar-wen's waist, "someday may it be filled."

The waterjar became heavy on her shoulders, and at the top of the next rise, she stopped to rest and breathe in the scent of the village spice gardens far below.

From here the round thatched roofs of the village looked like burrs on the smooth sinews of the valley foothills, but Marwen preferred the way the village looked in winterdark. Then the thatched roofs, glowing with firelight and light pouring from the east windows, looked like bleeding moons.

From further up the hill near Stumble Brook, Marwen could see two girls her age walking and sharing the load of their water-jars. She had played with Dalett and Lirca when she was younger, but they had run away from her since they were old enough to understand the word *soulless*. She watched them approach.

They didn't look at her. They circled around her and giggled and whispered. Marwen made her face still as stone and tried to swallow the dryness in her throat.

When they were past, she reached into her apron pocket and touched the Songbook, which contained all the spells and enchantments of Ve. While other children played, she had mastered the names of hill and stone more quickly than any other names, and the names of the grasses and the flowers, and the names of the waters: rain water and dew water, snow water and the water of Stumble Brook. Marwen whispered a brief spell. Lirca tripped on a rock and tumbled, spilling her water. Dalett cooed and comforted her friend, and shared her water with her. They didn't look at Marwen. They didn't suspect her. For them she didn't exist. Marwen wanted to cry out, "I did it! It was me, my magic." But she could not. She was voiceless, soulless. She was nothing, and her tricks meant nothing.

After they were out of sight, Marwen removed the book from her apron pocket, the leaves crackling with age. In the margins a poet, Grondil told her, had made hand drawings of dragons. She touched the drawings with her finger, traced them over and over. "Trouble up north," she had heard some of the villagers whispering lately, "dragon trouble." But others scoffed, for no dragons had flown in Ve for many generations. When Marwen was a little child, Grondil had often comforted her during Ve's long winters of darkness by assuring her that dragons only lived on the isles of the sea, far away from the shores of Ve. As Marwen gazed at the dragon drawings, the beasts frozen in fierce stillness, she thought that the poet had not imagined but seen, and she believed.

Nuwind passed and windsong began to blow. Greedily she read and memorized a few spells and enchantments that went beyond her level of learning. From the *Tenets of the Tapestry* every child was taught, but only the Oldwife read the *Songs of the One Mother*. Grondil, she knew, would be worried. "Too soon," she would say, "too much knowing and too little discretion." But Marwen could not stop herself. The words filled her up and gave her shape, and the empty places felt less empty. After a time a delicious sleepiness spread to her limbs, and she lay back on the grass. She could almost feel the world spin beneath her like a vast and immortal beast, and she wondered if it was for her, also, that the beast lived. Here in the wash of windsong she could find her magic. From the time she was a child, she had known this power, this passion that Grondil had taught her was called magic. It was her friend, a guide for one who had no tapestry, a soul for one who had no soul.

In Grondil's lap and before Grondil's loom, in Grondil's arms and in the arms of the magic, Marwen was god-given and talented, the magic's maiden, Grondil's only love. In Grondil's house or alone in the mountains, Marwen felt as big as a world, powerful and important and beautiful. But the moment she went into the village, she shriveled, her back stooped and she became awkward and stupid. When the villagers looked at her, they cast a spell with their eyes, and she became as small and insignificant as a dust mote, light and almost invisible, as empty and dark as her tapestry pouch.

Marwen opened her tapestry pouch. It wasn't completely empty. Carefully she took out a small stone she had found, almost perfectly round and blue as a summersun sky. She had shown it to Grondil who told her how it had been pushed and scrubbed and squeezed for a thousand years to be so round. If she had a tapestry, Marwen thought, it would have one blue thread the color of her stone. To wish for more would be greedy. She closed her eyes, rubbed its smoothness and tried to remember its exact shade of blue.

She felt a sudden pain as the stone was knocked from her hands. Marwen swallowed a cry and sucked hard on her knuckles.

"I might have knowed ye'd be idle, ya limpsy lollabed. Up! Up!" It was Cudgham Seedmaker, Grondil's husband. Marwen scowled at him. He was a goatish man who wore his shoes on the wrong feet when they wore out to make them last longer and who had a fair reputation for never having said a true word in his life. He and Grondil had often argued over her because he defended the village children who tormented her. Once Marwen had overheard him laughing as some adults told of their children's pranks against her. He had blamed it all on Grondil's method of upbringing. Of late he had taken an interest in her upbringing and sometimes found her alone in the hills.

"But my rock ..." Marwen said.

She saw it and reached for it, but a green and rust-striped ip lizard darted its tongue at her, and she drew her hand away quickly. She slid back slowly, not breathing, watching it, a lethargic creature, sun-loving and sleepy, deadly. This was a young one, its rust stripes stark against the green grass. Its eyes were like Cudgham's, Marwen thought, small and sly and black as mobbleberries.

"There be callers awaiting, girl. No time to waste. Ye must leave childish ways behind." He looked long at her from the height of his beast. "Ye are a woman now, aye, and an Oldwife's apprentice."

Callers! Perhaps someone needing her magic ... She climbed onto the beast behind him with one last look for her beautiful blue stone, but the ip lizard had curled its body around it. Cudgham balanced the waterjar before him, and Marwen put her arms around his girth.

"I always says to Grondil, 'Someday that girl will be a pester,' and now I see that I be a prophet," Cudgham said. "There now, hold close, girl."

Marwen said nothing, only closed her eyes and her nose against his presence.

In flight Cudgham stretched out his arm toward the northern wilderness, rolling and barren.

"Now there's a place where no man has placed his foot. I'd like to try my seeds in that soil, I would. Maybe I'll send Maug to test that soil." That Cudgham had chosen her cousin Maug as his apprentice was an insult to Marwen that still stung.

"He is not a seedmaker, he is a carver," she had protested.

"What good is that?" Cudgham answered. "He never makes anything."

Marwen had made that observation herself once in Maug's presence, and for that he seemed to hate her all the more.

She tried not to think about it. She thought how Cudgham had never left Marmawell in all his life, and she knew he never would. The villagers were content with their spice gardens and the living they brought. Let Buffle Spicetrader travel to distant cities to peddle their goods, the villagers had no such desire. They had no love for the wilderness hills. But Marwen gazed toward the desert hills and dreamed of dragons and how she would slay them.

The podhens burst into a flurry of feathers and squawks when they landed before the cottage, and Marwen by habit picked up an egg here, a handful of down there as she walked through the yard to the door. Grondil's hill goat nudged her at the doorway, and Marwen stopped to pull a burr from his beard.

"It's that useless girl of yours," she heard a nasal voice say. "Always off in the mountains, trifling away the hours with her tricks. Oh, yes, she can make the podhens lay black eggs, but I ask a simple spell of sharpening on my knives, and the dunderlass fails with her magic. Such a simple thing, Grondil, one you have done for me for years. I'll tell you what I think should have been in her tapestry—if you had made her one...."

Marwen listened in the shadow of the doorway until her hands trembled, and then she stepped forward.

The women looked up then in the dim light of the cottage. Grondil's eyes were large like blue wounds. Three other women sat in the room, too, village wives with cold porridge faces and eyes like dry stones.

"What do you say to this, child?" Grondil asked, her voice scarcely more than a whisper, as was proper for an Oldwife.

Marwen was sick of the *Tenets of the Tapestry* by which the Oldwives must live, forever servants to their people, using their magic in all meekness, and she was angry with Grondil. They are in Grondil's house, she thought, in my house, and here they cannot make me voiceless.

"Perhaps the spell missed the knife and sharpened her tongue instead," Marwen said quietly but clearly.

The women began to cluck, but Grondil silenced them with a gesture, her eyes steadily on Marwen. Marwen looked away first, shame blocking her throat. She approached Sneda, the woman who had been speaking. She had a large butcher knife in her lap, and Marwen took it in her hands.

She hated them all passionately in that moment, Sneda and the others for their bullish bossy ways and Grondil for her quiet acceptance. Perhaps that was why, as Marwen ran her finger down the blade of the knife, she was able so quickly to attune her mind to its cold still spirit, its essence of steel and silver that bade it be a knife, an instrument of blood and death. She spoke in its language, the language of hill and stone and hidden metals, of which she knew a little, and reminded it of its purpose and of its beauty in sharpness.

When she was done, her eyes focused on the three women, and she held out the knife in her two hands. "It is a good knife."

Sneda took the knife. Gently she touched the blade, and her brows arched, for blood dripped into her palm.

"Witch!" Sneda spat. Quickly she became alarmed, for the blood began to flow freely, and the women gathered around her, clamoring until Grondil covered the wound with an herb dressing.

The women left, their bodies and mouths rigid, the knife held gingerly by the handle.

"The magic is my friend," Marwen said softly to herself as she watched the three women through the east window. She smiled and spoke more loudly to Grondil. "With my magic I am this much bigger than Sneda and her old cronies." She made a huge gesture with her arm above her head.

"Bigger, perhaps," Grondil said, "but misshapen and ugly."

Marwen's mouth opened to speak and then slowly closed. Misshapen and ugly is better than invisible, she thought, but she couldn't say it aloud. Grondil was gathering herself, probably reciting all sorts of old tenets on containing one's anger, and she would expect Marwen, as her apprentice, to be doing the same.

For a long time after that, Grondil was silent, not because of any wish to punish her, Marwen knew, but because an Oldwife could not speak until she was in complete control of her emotions. They went about their duties, sweeping, cutting vegetables, mending, but Marwen worked distractedly and Grondil with obsessive concentration.

Finally Marwen could bear the quiet no longer, and as they sorted a tray of Cudgham's seeds, she said, "Why didn't you tell her you've hated using your magic for sharpening her nasty knives all these years. I should have turned her into an ip."

"I have loved you too much," Grondil said, her voice serene and hushed. She threw a bad seed into the fire. "The gods sent you to me. I was grateful for their gift and promised them that you would be theirs, and so I was lenient with you, protected you, indulged you." She looked at Marwen, but Marwen's eyes did not relent.

"The women are right. You are willful, and you speak of the magic with carelessness, as though it belonged to you and not you to it." She shook her head. "That is because you do not know the power you have."

Marwen was surly. "They don't respect you. They don't respect the magic."

"What need is there of respect?" asked Grondil, her palms to Marwen. "I trade my power for a living—is it to be held in more esteem than Sneda's shoemaking? Is the Spellsmith greater than the Blacksmith if there is a need for magic and metals? Those skills may be worthy of more honor, for the gift is given but the skill is acquired."

Marwen stared at her. Grondil had never sided with the others before. Since she was a child, Grondil had shielded her from the disdain of the villagers who called her a soulless one because she had no tapestry. And never before had Grondil told her of limitations or restricted her magic in any way.

She saw Grondil's forehead crease, worry darkening her skin like wingshadow. Marwen said, "I will not trade my art for shoes and pots. I will be a great and powerful Oldwife, and do great deeds of magic, and everyone will fear me."

Even in her own ears, the words sounded childish and hollow, but she narrowed her eyes and silently dared Grondil to laugh.

Grondil did not laugh. She folded her hands secretly like a wingwand folding her wings over her egg.

Marwen filled the embarrassing silence. "I shall do as Farrell in the *Songs of the One Mother*. I shall seek the Staffmaker, and he shall make me a staff, and I shall make wondrous magic. Perhaps I will find the wizard, and he will give me a soul."

Grondil's eyes filled briefly with light and then looked away. She sighed and seemed old to Marwen. "They say there is no wizard, Marwen, that the Songs are mere rhymes and fables." She was quiet for a time, her hands still.

Marwen knew what the people said and believed, but the Songs were more real to her than the people, and she remained steadfast. Grondil held her doubt in her heart like a stillborn child, a sadness ever to mourn and wonder. But with every word people spoke about the wizard being gone from Ve, Marwen felt that when she found him, he would be more entirely hers.

Grondil knelt before her and with her finger drew in the hard-packed dirt floor the shape of an hourglass.

"When you were a child," she said, "you thought, as I did when I was young, that as you grew in knowledge and magic, you would be able to do anything at all with your power. But see here—it is like the hourglass: the higher your powers, the narrower become your options to use it, for you come to know that every slight breath of magic moves the winds and the world. If you are gifted Marwen, you will go through this narrow opening. You will be frightened in that time to use your power at all. And then one day, the Mother grant it, everything will open up before you, and you will be free because you will not want to use your magic for anything but good."

Marwen heard her voice but not her words. She watched the thick-veined fine-boned hands that had woven many tapestries before Marwen's awed eyes, the quick and clever fingers that had patiently taught, over and over, the knots of the loom, that had taught her to make sophisticated patterns by transferring threads from one shed to another.

"Why?" she whispered. "Why, Grondil, was there no tapestry for me?"

Grondil eyed the east window, rose from the floor and sat on her stool. With one motion of her foot, she erased the picture in the dust, then tucked her feet beneath her sheath. Nervously she fingered something in her apron pocket.

"Without a tapestry, the people of the village felt you could be exempted from being given to the Taker. Some felt it may be an insult to the Taker to leave a soulless one. I have explained this to you before. But ..."

"But what?" Marwen asked. She had heard this "but" unspoken for years. Now for the first time Grondil had said it aloud. "But what?" she repeated.

Grondil could not answer her, for Sneda's youngest was at the east window and there was need in her eyes.

"Grondil, Oldwife of Marmawell, let your hands be blessed," the child said according to ritual. "Come with healing. My mother is hurt."

CHAPTER TWO

THE WINDOWS OF VE ARE LIKE EYES: YOU MAY
LOOK IN IF YOU WISH, BUT THEN YOU BEAR A
RESPONSIBILITY. —*TENETS OF THE TAPESTRY*

*E*VERYONE WHO had looked in at Sneda's window was there now, in or out of the house, their heads bobbing and weaving to see. Marwen could feel the eyes of the crowd on her back as she and Grondil passed through. They felt ungentle, but she had almost become used to that. It was the silence that was strange.

In the crowd was Maug who sneered and made jokes about Marwen whenever she passed so that all the boys laughed. It was he who dared Bero to throw an egg at her and he who had laughed Klawss to scorn when he was the only boy who danced with Marwen at the Sunrise Festival. It was Maug who made lewd remarks about her growing breasts. She felt small and stiff in her place beside Grondil, knowing his eyes were upon her.

Master Clayware was there, also, quiet and nearly hidden at the rear of the crowd, leaning upon a cane, his white hair cov-

ered by a dark hood, his spine curved. Since she was a child, he
had always had a kind word for Marwen, and once he told her
that her mother had been the most beautiful maid in the village.
Beside him, whispering in the old man's ear, was long-appren-
ticed Gumbe Clayfire whose blond hair hung in oily strands
around his ears and in his pale-lashed eyes. Gumbe was father to
Maug, husband to Merva Leatherworker, Marwen's aunt. Merva
had never forgiven the Council for allowing Grondil to keep her
sister Srill's baby, the baby who was her family's shame. Perhaps
that was why Merva had worked so hard recently to become the
head of the Council.

The villagers shuffled aside reluctantly for them. Sneda was
lying on the dirt floor in a pool of blood that still pulsed weakly
from the stump of her forearm where her hand had been. Beside
her lay the knife that Marwen had sharpened only hours before,
and next to that lay the white and lifeless hand that had been
amputated.

Sneda's oldest daughter, Leba, extended a dry chapped finger
and pointed at Marwen. "There's the weirdy witchett that hurt
my mother, the very one."

Marwen felt the unkind eyes of the people touch her like cold
fingers.

"Hush," Grondil said. She knelt, touched Sneda's face and
gently lifted the wounded arm. "Find me clean linen," she said
to Leba who stood biting her red raw hands until the cracks split
and bled. The girl went searching.

Leba was a leader among the girls Marwen's age, accepting
into her circle of confidantes only those select few who had a
measure of breeding or beauty or wealth. Leba had none of
these, but she had wisdom in the matters of people and knew at
a young age how to exercise her power. Marwen had never been

included in Leba's circle. One thing had saved Marwen's skin growing up, and it was that Leba and Maug hated each other more than they hated anyone else.

"This one is too late for spells," Grondil said. "But when magic fails, there is skill," and while Marwen stood frozen in place by cold eyes, Grondil worked. Once Marwen bent to help Grondil, but Leba hissed, and the cold eyes, like fingers, pulled her up, squeezed and pushed at her. Grondil did not seem to notice, but Marwen sensed that it was Grondil who kept the fingers from becoming fists.

The smell of blood was strong. Marwen gazed at the knife, touched it with her mind and searched for any evil she might have left without knowing. She felt gall rise in her throat. There in the essence of the knife, woven among its point and blade, was the anger that Marwen had felt for Sneda when she sharpened the knife. Quickly Marwen looked up, searching for some distraction that would ease her nausea. Only the grains of sand in the hourglass moved, sifting to the bottom of the glass. She remembered the *Tenets of the Tapestry,* its counsel that the Oldwife be at peace with all men and women.

A mumbling half-blind old woman was slowly working her way through the crowd to Sneda's feet. She was clothed strangely in a dress of rough green weel, clouted at the elbows and cuffs and tattered at the hem. Her apron, no less stitched and worn, was the blue of hot sky, with handprints of flour like clouds. On the old woman's feet were yellow slippers. In this tiny village, Marwen was sure she had never seen this grandmother in all her life, and yet no one else in the room seemed to take notice of her or even see her. Marwen could not stop staring at the old woman's face, her cataract eyes the color of ice, her skin falling like spidersilk, taut over the bones and drapey in the hollows.

"Who are you?" Marwen whispered.

The old woman did not speak, but she smiled sweetly at Marwen, nodded inanely and, with a wrinkled splotchy hand, made an arthritic pointing gesture at Sneda.

Grondil looked up and saw the old woman.

And then she did a thing Marwen did not understand at first. Though the *Tenets of the Tapestry* demanded that the Oldwife be soft-spoken and of gentle heart in all her dealings, never did they require that she be servile. Yet, before this old woman, Grondil bowed.

Leba began to wail.

Like an animal she howled, and two women put their arms around her and helped her to a bed. Marwen began to understand.

The old woman was leaning over Sneda with slow sore movements, smiling her blind smile and muttering and chuckling sweetly.

"The Taker?" Marwen said, her voice high and incredulous.

"Yes," Grondil whispered, and there was fear and warning in the stillness of her voice. Perhaps she knew, before even Marwen knew, what would happen next, too quickly for her to intervene.

Marwen picked up the cold blood-smeared hand, and just as the Taker bent to touch Sneda's foot, Marwen placed the severed member into the hands of the old woman. She was thinking of the eyes watching her use her magic to do glorious things that would earn her honor and love. She did not think of anything else. She placed her hands gently on the old woman's fragile shoulders, turned her around and led her out of the cottage.

The Taker mumbled and chortled like a village aunty, smiling and nodding, and all the while she cradled the hand in hers, as though it had an arm and a person attached. Outside, Marwen

let go of her shoulders and watched as the Taker shuffled around
to the other side of the house and vanished.

Marwen returned to Sneda's side and, putting aside Grondil's
hand, murmured the only spell of healing she had ever heard—
the simple words Grondil had said over her scraped knees and
stomachaches.

At once Sneda's skin became pink and her breathing more
regular.

"She is alive. The girl has saved her." The words spread like
wind, and in a moment the eyes were softer, and the coldness
was gone. Sneda opened her eyes and mumbled incoherently.
Amid sighs of relief, the eyes became decidedly warm.

But not Grondil's.

In her eyes were fear and pain, a breathless unbelieving pain
that she kept concealed from the people behind closed lips and
half-closed eyes.

Grondil said to the women, "She will need broth, warm and
wholesome. I will return to change the dressings." She turned
and left, Marwen following.

She would be very angry, Marwen knew. Grondil may even
punish her. But before Marwen left, she had met Maug's eyes,
and he had looked away in shame. Whatever her punishment, it
would be worth it.

When they arrived home, Grondil, in quiet calm movements,
began gathering articles of food to the center of the table: sud-
bread, dried fruit and waterphan.

Marwen stared. Her entire body began to prickle and sweat in
premonition.

"What are you doing? Are we going somewhere?" Marwen
asked. Grondil stopped and looked down, then resumed her
task.

"I am not leaving, Marwen. You are. You must."

The beating of her heart filled Marwen's head. She could scarcely hear Grondil over the sound of it.

"I'm sorry," Marwen said. She couldn't hear herself speak but she could tell Grondil had heard. "I'm sorry! What did I do? It was my fault that it happened, Grondil—I had to do something. I saved her life, didn't I?"

Grondil began gathering twine and utensils and blankets. "You saved her life, Marwen, yes. But it was all too late.

"Sneda will be an imbecile now, forever a burden to Leba, forever unable to care for herself. When the village sisters see what you have done, they will drive you away like an animal."

Marwen's shoulders shook. She forced her voice to calmness. "But you could stop them, Grondil. Please. Where will I go? Who will apprentice a soulless one? I don't want to leave." Marwen's voice got quieter with every word until it was no more than a desperate whisper.

Grondil did not answer. With strong articulate fingers, she rolled the food into a blanket and took twine to bind it.

"I won't go!" Marwen cried angrily. "You can't make me!"

Grondil jerked the rope into a knot.

"Mama!"

Grondil stopped. She did not look at Marwen but down at her hands. Marwen saw they were trembling and stared at them until Grondil stuffed them in her apron pocket where she fingered something nervously.

"It is not only because of Sneda, child," she said quietly. "You have robbed the Taker. She will be back. A life she was sent for, a life she will have, and now it will not be Sneda's life but another she seeks. The Taker is old, caring not for youth, and blind, caring not for beauty. You should have been the

Taker's baby, but I hid you from her. Now you have touched her, and she will know where to find you. But she can be slow. You will go. Soon. Now."

Grondil walked past her into the yard. A herd of wingwands grazed on the near slope and Grondil pointed.

"Of my three wingwands, I give you one. Choose your mount and return to me for your pack." The sun shone in her eyes clear as water. "I must give you something else before you leave."

"Who will apprentice me?" Marwen asked again weakly, but Grondil had already turned away.

She walked numbly toward the wingwand herd straggled on the slope, some eating, some sleeping, some uncurling their tongues into the shallow Stumble Brook. Grondil's house was on the outer yarding of the village, and so Marwen avoided passing all but Tamal Deathsayer's house. She stopped, remembering the day Grondil had cured his child's fever and how he had smiled at her that day. But not since. No one noticed her, for they were busy rethatching the roof, and the straw dust billowed like yellow smoke. She touched the house as she passed, the mud bricks warm as flesh. The wind on her face chilled her teeth, sucked at the hem of her shift.

"It is time I left," Marwen said aloud, so that her ears might agree with her mouth. "My magic has surpassed that of Grondil's. I have tricked the Taker. I will not cast spells on knives and kitchen gardens. I have heard Grondil sing of the wizard in her prayers, and if he is a fable, I will know of it before the Taker leads me to her land. Perhaps, for me, the wizard will have a seeing and give me a tapestry...."

Thus Marwen consoled herself until she was among the herd. The wingwands had never seemed so large before. They lifted their wings in the blowing wind and snorted against the grass. Three of them turned and walked toward Marwen. She stroked the wing of Sheerpaz, tickled the rough cere at the base of Broomstraw's antenna and ducked under Nightshade's enormous girth. She checked their shelljoints for parasites with an experienced eye.

The wingwands had become Marwen's friends when, as a child, she had played alone in the fields and hills. The creatures did not know that she was a soulless one, that she had no tapestry. At one time, when she had become aware of her magic and that it gave her power the other children did not have, she had used it to try and win the love of her peers. Then, instead of just fearing her, they also despised her. With time she had learned to embrace her loneliness and treasure it. Even so, there had always been Grondil and the wingwands.

It was a great thing to inherit a wingwand. Few families in the village owned one, and only the richest had two or three. In Marmawell their beauty was more prized than their usefulness. Only Trader Buffle ever used his beast to travel great distances, and it showed. The muscles at Peggypin's wingbase were thick and bulbous, and her left eye ran with green fluid from an infection, a bit of dirt that had cut into her eye when in flight. On the slope newborn Butterbug looked like a yellow sundewsie with its petals fluttering in the wind; his mother, Rue-the-day, catching the pink rays of the Morningmonth sun like a stempel-low in bloom, moved away from Marwen without alarm, calling her baby after her.

Plumbumble was Grondil's favorite and Rainbow, Cudgham's. Of Grondil's three, that left Opalwing. She had a long slender body, cream-colored, but her wings were her great beauty. Almost transparent, they fanned out like iridescent veils, shattering light into soft prism shards. Marwen had rarely ridden her, for she was young and somewhat skittish, but Grondil had told her long ago that one day Opalwing would be her own, that she had chosen her especially for Marwen, had sent Buffle Spicetrader on a long search for her. Marwen spoke softly in the beast's own language, and Opalwing sidled away. Again Marwen spoke to her, let the beast taste her skin, stroked her antennae until she was calm.

Marwen strapped on her pack, mounted, removed the stockings from Opalwing's antennae, and in a moment they were airborne. As a child Marwen had longed for the day she would be big enough to fly. She dreamed of the places she would go, of the freedom she would enjoy. But that first flight was brief, for there was no place to go, no hills as beloved as her own hills where she had named every cave and stream. From the air she could not savor every pretty stone or new flower or animal track. The feeling came back to her as she climbed toward the clouds.

Marwen circled back toward the village. She wondered what Grondil wanted to give her and resolved that she would not plead again to be allowed to stay. She would not cry.

Opalwing was descending when Marwen thought she saw someone walking westward into the hills. In another moment she was certain it was Grondil who walked so slowly. And in the next moment she banked Opalwing sharply in pursuit. For beside Grondil, hunched and nodding like an old village aunty, walked the Taker.

CHAPTER THREE

SING, SAD GRASSES IN THE HILLS 'NEATH THE SKY,
SING, SAD FLOWERLETS THE HOLLOW SPRINGS BY,
SING YOUR SONG OF DEATH FOR HERE THE TAKER HATH TREAD,
SING FOR THE LIVING AND NOT FOR THE DEAD.
—"DEATH SONGS" FROM *SONGS OF THE ONE MOTHER*

CULLERWIND WAS blowing when Marwen at last left searching the hills and landed Opalwing in the yard. There had been no trace of Grondil or the Taker when she reached the swell behind which they had disappeared, and though she drove the wingwand until her antennae quivered in fatigue, she did not find them.

Her knees buckled when she dismounted, and she leaned on the beast a moment before trusting her legs. A horror of entering the house filled Marwen. At last she rebelled at her fear and pushed the door open so violently that she startled three pod-hens to the roof. She stalked into the house. It was dim and quiet.

Grondil lay on the hearth floor, still as the dust beneath her, her face gray and unblinking. Marwen almost didn't recognize her without the lines of worry in her forehead. She looked as if she had gone quietly and obediently with the Taker. There was a shovel in her hand.

"Stop it," Marwen said. Her voice echoed slightly in the house. She fell to her knees beside the body. "Wake up!" A thin-wing crawled across the gray-blue lips.

She shook Grondil and shook her again.

"Nar rondillon, cu ondrega," she whispered fiercely, the spell that summons magic. Again she invoked in quiet fury. But if the magic came, it came in a form she did not expect, for beside her then stood Cudgham Seedmaker.

"What have ye done, ye addle-brained bratty? Have ye killed the Oldwife, too? Oh, Mother, what've ye done?" and he clutched his head and danced about the room in his wrong-sided shoes.

Marwen stared at him for a moment and then back at Grondil who lay so deeply still that she seemed to be sinking into the hard-packed dirt floor. A huge hard pain like a fist filled Marwen's stomach, and there was a cold silence in her head. She jerked her head toward Cudgham. "Stop it, fool! There was no love between the two of you—you married each other for convenience, and I have known it for years."

Cudgham stopped, his eyes narrowing.

"Convenience? What mean ye by convenience?"

"She married you that she might keep me, and you married her that you might have a warm house and prestige, deserving neither. Grondil spoke with me plain enough, you see, so don't put on your mourning for my benefit."

Cudgham took a step forward.

"Aye, ye've grown old and wise, haven't ye?" he said in his growling voice. "Practically a woman, ye be, 'tis true. Why did you kill her? Did ye want to be Oldwife yerself and sort my seeds all alone?"

He was looking at her strangely, his eyes hot as embers. Her upper lip drew back convulsively.

"I shall never sort your seeds again, Cudgham. I am leaving." She was afraid to be here without Grondil, afraid to be anywhere without a soul, but it would be worse here. She bent down to kiss Grondil's cold cheek. Cudgham bent over to stoke the fire.

"I know where your tapestry be," he said.

She had taken Grondil's lore books and was halfway across the room before the words meant anything.

"What?"

He was silent, stoking the fire.

"What did you say?"

"I know where your tapestry be. She told me a long time ago where it be hidden, in case anything happened to her."

Marwen dropped the books. A tongue of fire licked out toward her, then vanished, then licked out again. It burned behind Cudgham so that she could not see him clearly, only a dark hulk before the flames. "She told me I had no tapestry."

Cudgham looked away and rubbed his belly thoughtfully.

"You knew, and you have never disturbed it?" Marwen said.

"She threatened me with ... her magic, if I told. Or touched. I'll tell ye, if ye stay and cook for me, and sort my seeds. I be popular. May happen I can convince the village to accept ye as Old-wife. After all," he said coming close and touching her cheek with a thick smelly finger, "I am yer father. Promise me you will make me some magic, and I will show you where yer tapestry be."

After a long moment Marwen nodded, slowly, once. There was no thought of truth or lies in her, only desperation to see her tapestry. He smiled like a child and pointed at Grondil's body.

"It be there," he said happily. "She must have been digging

fer it." He rubbed his leathery head nervously. "If ye move her, I shall dig."

Marwen turned her eyes back to Grondil. She made herself look for a long moment. She could hear Cudgham breathing and the fire crackling and the wind sighing through the window. Outside, Opalwing twittered impatiently, and Tamal shouted over his roofing. Her hand fell to her side to where her tapestry pouch hung bright and new and empty.

"If this is another of your lies ..."

"I swear," he said. "I swear by the Mother."

She ground her teeth and dragged Grondil's body aside by her clothing. Already the dead woman's face had stiffened and the flesh had become cold, and she seemed to watch Cudgham with flat, dry, half-opened eyes. The dirt was hard as baked brick, and he was sweating profusely when he came to the tapestry.

The oilcloth around it was dirty but intact, and Cudgham held it out to Marwen unopened.

Her limbs would not work.

She sat, or fell, on the floor and held her head. She looked over at Grondil's body, not knowing if she wanted to kiss the pale cold face in the joy of having her tapestry or if she wanted to shake her for keeping it hidden all these years.

"Unroll it for me," she said.

From the back Marwen could see it was bright like a newborn's tapestry, that the colors were fresh and brilliant. Cudgham's eyes were wide and round, unblinking as he looked at it, and in his pupils were reflected the opulent designs, shining like varicolored flame.

"Let me see!" Marwen said. She held out her hands. "Is there anything of the magic in it?"

Cudgham's eyes narrowed. He looked at her as if he had forgotten she was there.

"No, nothing of the magic," he said. His voice was not happy any longer but gruff and choked. His head shone with sweat.

"Give it to me," she said, trying to stand up. "I don't believe you."

Cudgham's eyes flickered from Marwen to the tapestry and back to Marwen. He rolled up the tapestry clumsily and held it tightly in two fists.

"Ye promised," he said. "Ye said ye'd do for me—cook for me, clean and mend for me, and give me a little of your magic. Say ye promised."

Marwen stared at him for a moment. What he was saying seemed garbled like a foreign language. She felt herself gag.

"I must seek the magic," she said. "I know it is in my tapestry, give it to me!"

She lunged and felt Cudgham's heavy fist striking her face. She felt no pain. Her vision blurred, but what he did next, she saw clearly enough. In two movements he strode to the fire and thrust the tapestry into it. The threads were oily and aflame before Marwen could scream. She ran toward the fire feeling as though she ran in a dream, straining every muscle only to move as a bug in honey. Cudgham grabbed her from behind and was holding her. "Ye would have broken your promise if I'd given it to ye, I knowed it. But ye can make yerself another. I will be witness, if ye stay with me."

From the fire came a sound like hissing laughter as the flames devoured her tapestry.

Something snapped in her. With all her strength she freed one arm and raised it high.

"Dur! Moshe! Ip!"

She screamed the spell, a frightful sound in the house of Grondil who had never raised her voice.

Suddenly she was freed, and she turned.

Her eyes were blinded for a moment by the light of a new flame, and then she could see a thin column of green smoke rising from the body of a creature that crawled on the floor. She looked to the fireplace where the last of her tapestry was being consumed and back to the creature that crawled between her feet: an ip lizard, green and rust-striped, deadly poisonous.

A heavy lead-bone weariness enveloped her. She was strangely unafraid. She stroked the ip's dry rough back and touched its mouth. She picked it up by the tail, dropped it into her apron pocket and watched it roll itself into a leathery ball and go to sleep. It did not poison her as she thought it would.

CHAPTER FOUR

IN THE DARKNESS OF A SOUL'S WORST SOR-
ROWS ARE FOUND GREAT TREASURES OF SELF-
KNOWLEDGE, IF ONE HAS THE COURAGE TO
LOOK FOR THEM. —*TENETS OF THE TAPESTRY*

WHEN THE villagers found her, she was sifting through the ashes with the hearth-spoon, singing the spells of coming together and of finding, her face and hands gray with fine powder. Marwen did not seem to hear or see them and did not resist when they forced her to come away.

They laid hands on her and brought her before the Council, a group of village women who sat in a row like podhens on a roof. Marwen sat on the ground before them, rocking gently and whispering the words of a spell over and over. All around her, at a respectful distance, were gathered the villagers, some laughing and some talking angrily among themselves. The children played chasing games, and mothers passed out sweets to bribe them into stillness. The laughter of the children began to draw Marwen out of her trance. As she surfaced, a squeezing pain in her upper chest gripped and grew more intense until it seemed it would suffocate her.

Lirca and Dalett were whispering and staring at her with wide-eyed fascination. Into the village yard, Leba had her mother, Sneda, carried, where she lay drooling and moaning. Leba's face above her was full of malevolence.

Gumbe Clayfire stood with his arms across his huge stomach and triumph in his smile. Only Master Clayware looked sad and older.

Maug stood apart from the crowd, tossing and catching rocks that, when he missed, fell close to Marwen.

The Council head rose, and everyone gradually fell silent.

"Marwen, apprentice to Grondil, this Council has been called to accuse you. You will listen, and before we pass sentence, you may speak."

The Council head was Merva Leatherworker, sister to Srill. She rarely spoke to Marwen except when Marwen came to cast spells on her kitchen garden, and when she did speak, she would often smirk and say, "You look nothing like your mother. Pray you have not her evil heart as well." Now she looked pleased, as though it were a great relief to have this opportunity to vindicate her family's shame.

"You are accused of using your magic to a dark end, Marwen: that is, the living death of Sneda Shoemaker. You are also accused of the death of Grondil Oldwife. Let the witnesses testify."

One by one members of the village came forward: the women who had seen Marwen cast the spell on the knife, the many who had heard Marwen and Grondil whispering the Taker's name and Leba who reported her mother's condition in great detail. When Merva spoke again, her voice was calm. "It is obvious to me that the Taker came to retrieve the life that you robbed, and somehow you tricked her, tricked her again into taking Grondil's life instead of your own," Merva said.

The villagers all murmured their agreement. One of Maug's rocks fell on Marwen's back with a soft thud. "I could turn you into an ip," Marwen thought. "I could turn you all into..." Just then a man came running to Merva and whispered something to her. She looked at Marwen.

"Where is Cudgham Seedmaker, girl?"

Marwen felt Cudgham-ip's warm heaviness in her lap, sleeping as he was in her apron pocket. Horror at the enormity of her deed chilled her. It was true. She was soulless, an empty shell with no purpose at all on Ve save to cause hurt at every turn.

"I do not know where my stepfather is," she whispered.

Leba's voice screeched near her. "Liar! You have probably killed him, too. I have seen you repel his attempts to be an affectionate father. Do witches have hearts?" She spat on Marwen's face.

Marwen felt the saliva slide down her cheek, warm and thick. It was true, she was a liar. But she did have a heart. She knew she did, for it was heavy and swollen in her breast, and she knew it must burst at any moment. She sat in the dust unmoving.

Merva was speaking again, but Marwen did not hear. Remembering the *Tenets of the Tapestry,* she whispered a brief spell for help and understanding. She looked up at the villagers. One by one she looked into their eyes, and this time she saw what lay raw behind them: fear. They were afraid of her, they had feared her power as a child and the power she would have as Oldwife. But more than that, they feared her as a soulless one, as one born without a tapestry.

A glimmer of hope flashed in the wash of her despair like a bright fish swimming upstream in Stumble Brook. She was not soulless. Not anymore. She had a tapestry, Grondil had made her a tapestry after all. One who lost the tapestry and who died before it could be remade was destined to be lost or to suffer in the lands of the dead. But suffering was better than not existing at all, she thought. She looked around at the villagers, compassionate in her new hope. In her they saw all the dreadful possibilities of their own lives. She thought of Grondil, gentle as she touched a sore with her finger, and her heart swelled so full there was no room left for hating.

"And so, Marwen, by law, you have the opportunity to speak," Merva was saying, each word like the crack of knife against bone. "Begin."

Marwen stood. She wiped the spittle from her face, but it mixed with the ash and streaked her skin with two black stripes. She looked over to the hills and garnered strength. Perhaps her tapestry had a spirit of its own, perhaps if they killed her, she would find it while she wandered in the dead hills.

"I—" She stopped. She looked into the faces of the crowd, her throat closed tight and finally her eyes fell on the kindly old face of Master Clayware. People were not like stones, she thought numbly, becoming smoother with the squeezing and scrubbing of years. Master Clayware's face was as wrinkled and folded as dried fruit. She looked into his eyes and spoke. "I do have a tapestry," she whispered. There was a shifting in the crowd but the faces did not soften. The silence swelled up like a bubble, and Leba broke it with a hissed, "Liar!"

"But it's true. It's true!" Marwen cried. "And there is something wonderful in it—wonderful enough to frighten Cudgham. So he burned it. Grondil made it for me after all, but she hid it so that you wouldn't..." Her words were tumbling over one another like rolling pebbles, and she forced herself to stop and breathe. "I'm sorry. The *Tenets of the Tapestry* says that no one has an enemy without a cause. I should have tried to understand, I should have served...."

There was shuffling and coughing throughout the crowd, and a woman began to make a fuss over her child. Someone pushed Marwen back down into the dirt.

Merva lifted a hand to the people.

"Silence!" Her head, neck and back were as straight and stiff as a drying pole. "Your 'shoulds' are eloquent Marwen, but they will not recover the past. Your sentence is banishment to the northern wilderness without beast or bag. The Taker shall decide if you live, as she should have done at your birth. So be it."

Marwen listened. She felt lighter, as if relieved of a burden. Her tapestry was gone, but fate was mindful of her and would force her steps for a little while at least.

Maug and two of his friends, Bero and Japthas, stepped forward. Merva smiled at them and then at Marwen, benignly.

"These young men have volunteered to see to the task. Take her."

Maug approached her with a rope.

"Do not bind me," Marwen said, her fingers clutching at the dust. "I will go willingly."

Maug looked at Merva who nodded her head slightly. While Maug stood there, Master Clayware stepped forward to speak. The crowd murmured, but Merva could not silence Marmawell's most respected citizen.

"Do not bind her," he commanded in a quavering voice. Maug hesitated, then dropped the rope, and after a silence Master Clayware continued speaking. "The sentence has been passed, but I would ask you to consider: Buffle Spicetrader has brought news of a dragon in Ve, heading west from Verduma. Without Marwen, without an Oldwife, we are defenseless."

Some of the younger people smirked, and someone laughed aloud. But most people glanced anxiously at the sky, and the children ran to their mothers.

"Dragons?" Merva said in a condescending tone. "I do not believe in dragons anymore than I believe there is a wizard, Master Clayware."

The old man nodded patiently. "Believe what you will. In the old days, we listened in faith to the Songs, and we were happy. Grondil's grandmother told me herself before she died that she had seen the wizard and believed. This child, though—will you not for Grondil's sake be more lenient? As a child she obeyed the laws perfectly, excelled in letters, and spoke of the wizard with passionate innocence. You thought she held herself above you, you thought she rejoiced in her superiority, and so you despised her and ostracized her. Do you not take any responsibility for the misuse of what is obviously a great gift of magic?"

Merva answered in a loud voice, her composure gone. "If her magic is great enough to save us against dragons, let her save herself!" She looked at Marwen. "Return to us, and I will reconsider your fate, but the wilderness is a place that cares not for little girls' tears. The Council is ended."

She turned and walked away.

"I didn't cry," Marwen called after her, and she thought Merva's step faltered.

In a few moments, the entire crowd had returned to their work and their play, leaving Marwen alone except for the three young men and Master Clayware. The old man opened his mouth, then closed it again.

The three young men mounted wingwands, and Marwen was

instructed to ride behind Maug. He smelled sour, and there were pimples on the back of his neck. She hung on to the wingwand's shell rather than put her arms around him, but the take-off jolted her and she grabbed on to his shirt. He turned his head toward her.

"Don't be shy, witch. If you think I'd fancy an ugly like you, you are wrong."

Master Clayware raised one hand, and Marwen thought he would have called them back if he could.

They flew north into the desert hills where few streams ran, and the predominant inhabitants were insects and ips. She thought of Opalwing waiting without socks on her antennae, able to fly, and she called out to her with her mind but without hope. She was not afraid of the wilderness, but the immortal hills could be harsh with those of the world who needed food and water to survive.

At some point Marwen fell asleep, for she awoke as she was pushed off the wingwand, still too groggy to steel herself against the fall. It was freshwind. Maug, Bero and Japthas loomed over her, silently, their eyes shifting. Marwen scrambled to sit up, but Maug pushed her back down with his foot and held her there, his weight on her chest. She could smell wingwand manure on his boots.

"You may be a witch, but you are also getting to be a woman," he said, "though a scrawny homely one. I think she should grant us a wish, don't you boys?"

Bero laughed, and he and Japthas punched each other. Marwen struggled to breathe against the weight of Maug's foot, but she did not try to sit up. She felt a coldness in her throat and stomach, as though she had swallowed a large stone. She was still, her eyes locked on Maug's eyes. They were as hard and

shallow as mirrors, and in them she was tiny as an insect. He lifted his boot from her chest and toed her spidersilk further up her
thigh.

She forgot her speech to the villagers about understanding.
She reached into her apron pocket and drew Cudgham-ip out by
the tail.

The boys staggered a few paces back, their eyes full of wonder
and terror.

Marwen sat up, swallowing air.

"Aye, you should be afraid but not only of ip poison. For
this, Maug, is Cudgham Seedmaker, my stepfather." Marwen
could not keep her voice from shaking. Even with all the magic
in the world, she would be afraid of Maug who had another
power, one she did not understand, a shrinking power. She
watched their confidence crumble a little with only a slight less-
ening of her fear. She crawled forward, shaking the ip at them.

"You hag!" Maug screamed as he and the others ran to their
mounts. "I hope you die in these hills like you should have when
you were born!"

She watched them fly away until they were mere blemishes on
the cloud-stippled blue of the morning sky.

CHAPTER FIVE

BELIEVE IN YOURSELF, IN LOVE, IN THE GOOD OF OTHERS BUT, MORE IMPORTANTLY, BELIEVE IN THE MAGIC, FOR IN THIS THERE IS POWER TO OBTAIN ALL OTHER BELIEFS. —*TENETS OF THE TAPESTRY*

COLD AND hunger were hard upon her waking moments when Marwen emerged from a black sleep. She lay still for a time, cradled in the earth's arm. Above her the roof of the little hollow in which she had found shelter was filled with bared roots dangling like exposed nerves. The hollow seemed to have been scraped by some bisor beast that wandered these round and rolling hills. Further out Marwen could see that the hills became more muscled, with overhanging rocks protruding from the crests like brows.

She stood up. On the gold-grassed slope above her was an oldman rock, well-bearded with moss, pocked and splotched with age. She picked up a pebble and placed it at the foot of the rock.

"Venerable one, have you any words of wisdom for me?"

She waited long in silence.

"You are slow to answer. You must be wise." She placed another pebble at the base of the rock. "You see, grandfather rock, I am Marwen who knows not the name of her father and whose mother has twice died." A picture of Grondil walking with the Taker filled her mind, and she forced the thought away. "I have no tapestry, and that is bad. It is the worst thing that can happen, and it also has happened two times."

Marwen was quiet then, listening. The rock did not invite her to touch it, so she listened.

Presently she heard the whisper of rushing water. "I must listen for the water," she said quietly. "That is your answer." The sound of running water was coming from far off, and after following the sound for a time, she found a tiny stream pouring like a bit of white lace from a lip of rock. She drank deeply and then followed the stream down into a shallow ravine that eventually led to a stream of shoals and shallows, more rock than water.

Opalwing was there on the bank, drinking.

Marwen ran to her, crying out. She wrapped her arms around the wingwand's head and stroked her antennae, but the beast butted at the grass and swung its head so that Marwen laughed and let go. "It is a sign," she whispered. She looked into the faceted eyes of the wingwand and saw herself broken into a hundred tiny selves, looking out as if from behind glass. "A sign, yes," she said. "And I wonder why Grondil searched so long and far for you that she might give you to me—Grondil who never wasted an hour or an ounce of anything in her life." She stood stroking the beast's backfur distractedly until the wave of grief was gone, and she realized that she felt hungry and dirty.

Marwen stripped off her spidersilk and stepped into the water. In only a few moments, her feet and ankles ached with the cold. Clenching her jaw she lay down on the pebbly bottom, leaning her head back until only her face was above water. The water carried her hair downstream. When her breath was coming in gasps, she ducked all of her face beneath the water.

She emerged like a silver fish that flings itself on the bank and then heaves and mouths for breath. She pulled her spidersilk over her head, and as she did so, the ip fell out of her pocket and righted himself with slow snaky movements.

"Oh, Cudgham!" Marwen said. "I'd almost forgotten. Why, you are almost as loathsome and stupid a reptile as you were a man." She put crossed fingers to her lips and frowned. "If Grondil heard me say that, she would make me read ten pages of the *Tenets* out loud for punishment."

She looked around.

"What do you eat? Can I catch you a nice slimy slug or a many-legged insect perhaps?"

The ip answered by darting out his long tongue and capturing a jimmie, which it rolled into his mouth and swallowed whole.

"Ooo," Marwen half-grimaced and half-gloated. "Wouldn't it be fun to turn you back into a man while the bug is still in your belly."

She took a deep breath and uttered the reversal of the spell. Nothing happened. There the lizard sat, unchanged and blinking with slow transparent eyelids. She tried again, again nothing.

Marwen shrugged, almost relieved. Just to be sure, she snapped her fingers once. She had meant to turn him blue or black, but she had never been able to snap her fingers very well. The ip turned a dainty shade of pink.

She covered her mouth with her hand to stifle a giggle and then forced her face to be serious. "No, that is too cruel," she said, and she turned him back to his green and rust color.

"Well, perhaps the wizard can tell me the proper spell. All the more reason to find him." Talking out loud about the wizard, a thing forbidden in Marmawell, made him seem more real to her, and she took heart. "Nevertheless, should you bite me, Cudgham, you shall be left like this forever. Do not forget." The creature blinked again.

Opalwing was grazing morosely on the tough yellow stubble. "You are hungry, too, aren't you?" Marwen said. "There is nothing but this dry wiregrass for you to eat and less still for me to eat."

Her stomach rumbled as she looked around at the hills that spread from horizon to horizon. She could remember little of the few maps she had seen. She knew that Ve was surrounded by water on all sides, and most of the villages were nearer the coast where the soil was rich enough and the rain frequent enough to grow food. Marmawell was different from other villages because it was situated more inland where the soil was drier. There they grew the spices for which Marmawell was famous. The major trading cities, including Kebblewok, were more central, but even with Opalwing, it was too far a journey without provisions.

Marwen felt a chill of fear. Not even with magic could she produce food from nothing. She could, if she could remember the spell, make the wiregrass look and taste more appetizing. But it would still be wiregrass and could not sustain her long. She sorely wished that she had brought her *Tenets* and her *Songs of the One Mother*. They were her inheritance, precious treasures that Grondil would have given her on her deathbed.

Marwen remembered Merva Leatherworker's words: "Return to us, and I will reconsider your fate...." True, Merva had not thought that Marwen would have a wingwand, but was that not a result of Marwen's own magic? Had she not summoned the creature with her mind? Her magic was enough to save her, and besides, she needed to return for her books whether Merva allowed her to stay or not. Books and provisions: for these she would risk a second exile. And maybe, Marwen thought, maybe I shall not stay anyway, even if they allow it.

She stood. "Come, Opalwing, let us go. The dead are not served by our fasts." She picked up a moss-slicked pebble from the river bottom, and ran and gave it to the oldman rock.

"Thank you, grandfather stone, for now my thoughts are as clear as the water. I shall return to the village and beg forgiveness. I will search among Grondil's books until I find the words to return Cudgham to his former state and get him to stand witness at a tapestry making, my tapestry making."

Marwen dug up a few stickstem roots from the bank of the stream and without magic made a small fire over which she roasted them. She pierced the outer hull and ate the soft meat inside, which, though bland, was filling and warm. It gave her strength to begin her flight back to Marmawell.

Freshwind was gentle in the constant sunlight of spring and summer, though in winterdark it often brought freezing rains from over the sea. Opalwing flew evenly into the saltsoft breeze, seemingly glad to be headed home. Her wings met at the top and the bottom during flight, as the wings of all well-bred wingwands do. Marwen filled with a lovely dizzying sensation of height at every wingbeat as the ground below was first hidden, then revealed.

About a third of the way to Marmawell, Opalwing began to slow her speed. When Marwen urged her to fly faster, the beast balked and reduced her speed even more. Opalwing was young and unused to flying long distances, Marwen knew, so she allowed the creature to land and graze for a time. While she waited for her to rest, Marwen noticed an unusual cloud in the south.

"What is that, Opalwing? Is it a storm cloud? Is that what makes you nervous?" she asked. But after the beast had eaten and slept, she still would not fly. Marwen cajoled and pushed and shouted, but Opalwing would not budge. There was little else she could do. A wingwand could throw its rider for mistreatment received years before. It was better to humor the powerful intelligent creatures. Finally Marwen herself slept.

The cloud had disappeared when Marwen awoke, and Opalwing willingly resumed the journey. Occasionally she changed direction nervously, as though she smelled a predator, and it took all Marwen's skill and strength to steer her back on course.

When they were close to Marmawell, though still beyond sight of it, Opalwing landed without warning and without direction to do so. She almost unseated Marwen and then disobeyed Marwen's commands to fly. Finally, in frustration, Marwen punched the hard shell of the creature's body.

"I should let Cudgham-ip nip your heels," she said, close to tears. She was hungry and thirsty and sore from sleeping on the ground, and she knew Marmawell was just beyond the next hump of hills. She started to walk, stopping to look back occasionally, but the wingwand did not follow.

She had not walked far when a smell made Marwen's heart pulse in her throat. It was a nauseating stench that drove away all thoughts of food. On the wind were shreds of black smoke like ghosts blowing by.

For two more winds she walked. She had her first sighting of the village at cullerwind. Cullerwind in winterdark often brought hail or blizzard or windwraiths—those freakish phantom winds that inexplicably tore the roof from one house or bore away one podhen out of an entire flock. In summerlight, however, culler-wind was usually benign, its worst deed winding the clothes round and round the drying poles until they looked like strange heavy fruits on an unnatural vine.

But there were no wadded clothes, no drying poles, no people, no huts. Nothing. Marmawell was gone, and in its place was a black stain on the loins of the hills.

The hills did a half-turn before her eyes, and she struggled to maintain her footing. A muscle in her temple twitched. Time and place lost all landmarks by which she understood them. She was unsure if this charred valley was really the place where her village had been, though looking more closely she could see parts of huts still standing. She was unsure how long she had been in returning, though the position of the sun told her it had been little more than a cycle of winds. She even doubted the events of the past few days and thought perhaps it had all been part of a hideous dream.

She peered into her apron pocket. Cudgham-ip slept, and she touched his leathery hide, as though she were touching reality itself.

"By the Mother!" she whispered. Where before a herd of wingwands had grazed, only a few charred lumps remained like blisters on the hillside. A summer windwraith scooped up some black dust and whirled it into the sky along with a feather and a strand of straw. But for the wailing of the wind in Marwen's ears, there was complete silence.

She walked heavily toward the half-burnt remains of what had been her own hut. Halfway into the valley, she came upon a body. It reminded her of the clay dolls the little village girls made, dark and shriveled imitations of people. She opened her mouth to sing the Death Song, but no sound would come out.

After a while she continued walking. The wailing of the wind sounded more humanlike the closer she came to the hut.

Nothing was left standing but part of one wall. She saw that it had not been burned but crushed and that a number of other huts in the village still stood in various degrees of ruin. Then it was that Marwen heard a voice above the wind, a familiar voice, Maug's voice.

For a moment she almost turned and ran. But she did not. A human voice, even if it be Maug's, was a welcome sound. She rounded the wall and peered into the shadow. It was Maug, but his back was to her, and he was standing beside someone, someone whose low moans mingled with the wind's sighs. It was Master Clayware.

The old man's white beard had been burned away, and the brown leathery skin of his face and neck was swollen and pearly white. He was struggling for breath, but when he saw Marwen, it was seemingly without surprise. He held out his charred hand to her and beckoned.

Maug looked behind him and jumped as if he had been bitten. "You! How did you—?"

She did not look at him but knelt at the side of Master Clayware on the dirt floor.

"Tell me what happened," she said.

He answered with a single word: "Perdoneg." His breath whistled and wheezed, and Marwen could see he was dying.

"The dragon's name is Perdoneg," Maug said. He sounded as if the air had been knocked out of him. "I was digging Grondil's grave, and Master Clayware was singing the Death Song beside me when he came. We hid in the grave—we could hear the people screaming.... Finally Master Clayware could bear it no longer, and he came out. He was burned.... The dragon ate some of the people.... I saw ..." There was a strange joy in his voice, though the skin around his mouth was white.

"Is anyone else left alive?"

Maug shook his head. He was looking at her with wild gleaming eyes, but she didn't think of him. She turned back to Master Clayware. The magic was rushing through her body like wind in a tunnel, roaring in her ears, demanding to be used. For the first time, the magic had come to her unsought and unbidden, and she learned much about the magic in that moment.

"I would relieve your pain," she said.

"No pain," the old man said, "but for that which is in my heart."

"Let me help you," she said.

He nodded, a faint but sure movement. "You will help me, but not in the way you think, Marwen. The gods have brought you back so I might give you a message." The old man spoke with a huge effort of will.

"Years ago a man came to our village and stayed all during winterdark. A poet he was, silver-tongued and well-learned, with a singing voice that made the old ones weep and the young girls dream. He was witty and charming and looked as though he hadn't a care in the world until ... until your mother and he fell in love."

The wind blew some charred dust into Marwen's eyes, and she held her breath against it. "Was the poet my father?" she asked.

Master Clayware nodded. "How I wish he were here now to sing my Death Song."

Above the stench of burned flesh, the wind blew into her nostrils the sweet scent of roast spices. Hadn't she known it all along? Perhaps it was the way Grondil had looked at her when she spoke of him or the sadness in her voice when she sang a Song she had learned from him. Or perhaps the dragons he had drawn had spoken to her. "Why has he never come for me?" she asked.

"Child, you know that in Ve no weddings may be performed during winterdark and not a day sooner than Sunrise Festival. Srill and her lover begged the Council to forgo this tradition and marry them because he had a quest to fulfill, a deadly quest from which he knew he may not return. The Council rejected their pleas. Merva especially incited the Council against it, though it seems to me her first child came early." The old man seemed to have forgotten that Maug was there.

"Grondil was young then. She looked with disapproval on the light-minded ways of this man, and she would not speak against the decision of the Council."

He stopped to catch his breath. Marwen breathed with him, willing his lungs to take in air. The skin on her arms and back prickled.

"But the man boarded with me and was kind to me, and at last I could bear his pain no longer. As a member of the Council, I married them secretly, though how legal it was, I know not."

The old man looked over at Marwen. His eyes were nearly swollen shut and his words came garbled and rasping from his burned lips.

"I tell you this so you may be comforted. Perhaps I should have told you long ago. But my message is this: before your father went away, he told me that he had conceived a child, that it would be a girl.... I shall never forget his face. All the laughter and levity was gone, it was as though he had been wearing a mask all that time and beneath the mask was a countenance full of wisdom and sorrow."

The old man swallowed three times.

"He asked me to care for Srill and the child she would bear, for, he said, Srill will know what to teach her. But, he said, if the gods be so unkind as to take Srill away, tell my daughter to seek my home in Verduma, for in it is the dragon's tapestry."

The old man closed his eyes. Marwen waited, feeling as though her life and all its events were funneling to this point, to these strange words that Master Clayware spoke at his death.

"I thought, years later, when you were but a child and the charm of the man had worn from me with the years, that perhaps he had been mad. I thought that if dragons lived, it was far away across the sea. I thought how odd you would think me if I were to give you such a message. But now, I have seen. Eyes—spinning eyes full of knowledge and hate, and wings—wings of such expanse that I could not see them all in one glance. And claws and teeth ... ah, ah, where is the Taker? She stays so long!"

"Master Clayware, what was my father's name?"

The old man sighed and looked past her, as though he were seeing someone, an old friend. He smiled a little, though on his face it became a grimace.

"Nimroth," he said. "Your father's name was Nimroth."

CHAPTER SIX

AT THE ONSET OF WINDEVEN, MASTER CLAY-
WARE DIED. —FROM THE *TALES OF MARWEN OF
MARMAWELL*

MARWEN DID not see the Taker. It is said that sometimes the spirit leaves a broken body before it is invited to do so, and then it must wander the hills in confusion until the Taker comes and leads it away to the lands of the dead.

Marwen sang the Death Song for Master Clayware. She sang it for Grondil, and for Leba and Sneda Shoemaker, and for Srill, her mother. She sang and sang until her voice would no longer make any sound. Then she slept.

When she woke, Cudgham-ip was basking in the sunlight near her face. Her tongue was swollen and dry in her mouth, and it was difficult to swallow.

"Is that really Cudgham?" Maug asked. He was sitting nearby, carving a piece of black bone and watching the creature's every move.

Marwen sat up and moved away from him. "I need water," she croaked.

He looked at her oddly, deliberated for a moment and then disappeared. She stood and began searching for Grondil's lore books amidst the rubble of the hut. When Maug returned with fresh water, she had found the *Songs of the One Mother*. Even before she drank, she opened it and with renewed fascination touched the dragon drawings in the margins. For me, she thought, my father drew these for me.... She closed her book, eyeing Maug. Keeping him in her sight, she drank deeply, though the water tasted of cinders. Again she opened the book. At last she came upon some spells of restoration. With her hand upon Cudgham-ip she spoke them, one after another, to no effect.

Maug watched her without speaking.

Finally she stood, put the ip and the book in her apron pocket and began walking to the hills where Opalwing was waiting.

At the top of the hill, she looked back to see her village for the last time. Maug was following her. He did not try to hide, and she waited for him.

Where his brass-colored hair touched his face there was a line of pimples, and below that his pale blue eyes were wet and red-rimmed.

"Don't go without me," he said.

"Why would you want to come with an ugly like me?" she asked.

Maug looked down and shrugged, and Marwen felt ashamed. To leave him here without a wingwand was to sentence him to death. He made an odd sound, and Marwen thought perhaps he was weeping.

"I have no tapestry," he said.

She stared at him.

"When the dragon came, I was digging Grondil's grave. It was fitting to take off my tapestry pouch," he said.

"It was burned in the fire?"

He nodded. "You saw it once, Marwen, my cousin, not many years ago. You could stand as witness for me."

"Yes, I remember. You were taunting me, and you dangled it in front of me." She remembered vaguely the images of a star, a floxwillow and a spoon.

He looked at his feet and shrugged again.

"Of course, I don't remember it," she said, "but it is only a moderately difficult spell to bring it to mind." She looked directly into his eyes, feeling herself turn pink. "If I wanted to."

"By the gods, Marwen ..."

"Now you know how I feel!"

His lips twisted scornfully. "It's not the same at all. I will have neither work nor friends until my tapestry is remade, and I must be careful not to die. But you—you are soulless."

Her throat closed around her protests. He had no reason to believe her, and it was enough for her just to know that she did have a tapestry and a soul.

"I will not tell," Maug said, "if you promise that the first Oldwife we come to, you will witness my tapestry."

She nodded, and with that pact they began to walk the tawny hills inland.

At nuwind they came upon Opalwing butting and pawing hungrily at the wiregras   "So that's how you got back so fast," Maug said. "Thought you might have used magic." He snorted, and Marwen resisted the urge to strike him. She turned to him, chin and chest thrust out.

"I'll sit forward," she said. "You may hold on however you wish. Just don't touch me."

"Gor, who'd want to," he retorted but without conviction, as if he didn't even care enough to fight with her.

With the roughest start Marwen could get out of Opalwing, they began their journey toward Kebblewok.

When they stopped to give Opalwing a rest, Marwen roasted some stickstem roots, which Maug devoured peel and all. They had salvaged two jars of oatbeer and some burned bread from the ruins, but they were saving them. For a long time, they did not speak, though Marwen smiled at him once or twice. Whether she was afraid of him or whether she had some childish need to have him like her, she did not know. When he finally spoke, she started a little.

"Where are we going?" he asked.

She tried to hold the food in her cheek so that she could speak with her mouth full. "Grondil told me once that if I kept the rising sun to my right and the norwind blowing into my face, that I should come to the city of Kebblewok."

He nodded. "And then?"

Marwen let the dry nutty-tasting meat of the root slide warm and heavy down her throat. She did not know where she was going. Her future spread out before her like the endless rolling hills on either side, without lane or landmark. Grondil was dead, and now, strangely, she longed for her father, Nimroth, who had loved her after all. She felt stripped of purpose. All that was left was her strange inheritance, the dragon's tapestry. But before that she must have her own.

"I will go to the Oldest in Loobhan. Perhaps she can help me discover the spell to change Cudgham back so he can witness my tapestry. And after that I think I shall seek my father's house," she said. Nimroth—a strange name, she thought, one I have never heard before.

Maug looked at her shrewdly. "You don't believe that stuff, do you? Master Clayware's babblings? Surely he was delirious."

Marwen coughed as some of the root went down the wrong way. When she recovered herself, she said, "You do not believe?"

Slowly, deliberately, his eyes full upon Marwen, he shook his head.

It was while they were eating that they felt a charge in the air, as though a storm were gathering. Marwen looked about her. The sky toward the sea was glowering, but in the east the sun lay like a pink egg in a nest of golden clouds. Below it the land was barren.

She ignored the feeling for a time as she ate, but when the hair on her forearms raised, she jumped up, dropping her root. She looked around for Cudgham-ip, but he was a little way off, near where Opalwing grazed. Then Marwen saw her. The Taker.

Her head was bent, her white hair like bits of cloud or cotton. Her apron glowed brilliant blue like a shred of summer sky, the stitches of patchwork like birds in flight far off. As she walked with halting deliberation toward Marwen, she muttered and mumbled and chortled incoherently.

Marwen felt bile burning in the back of her throat. "Go away, old woman!" she called. Maug jumped up.

The Taker lifted her head, though Marwen could tell she saw little. She laughed sweetly and waved with stiff spotted fingers.

"No, go away!" Marwen screamed. "Is not Grondil's life enough? Is not a whole village enough to fill you?"

The old woman shuffled on, reaching out her arms toward Marwen as if she would embrace her. Marwen began stepping backward, then turned and ran. Maug ran beside her until they reached Opalwing. Marwen's fingers shook as she pulled the stockings from the wingwand's antennae. Maug had already mounted and given the signal to fly before Marwen had a chance to mount.

But the wingwand did not move. Marwen jumped on in front, too frightened to be angered or repulsed by Maug's arms reaching around her waist.

"Fly, Opalwing, fly!" She pushed her hands cruelly into the space between the beast's head and body shells.

Then the wingwand's legs buckled and they had to jump from her back to avoid being pinned as the beast collapsed.

"Opalwing!" Her terror turned to disbelief and anger, for attached to Opalwing's leg, still venting its swift venom, was the creature Cudgham-ip.

Marwen wrenched it off by the tail. "Anything, so as not to be left behind?" she hissed.

Then the sound of the old woman's wheezing breath was behind her, and without looking back Marwen ran, still holding Cudgham by the tail. Maug, gasping for breath, ran beside her.

Marwen ran until her legs were heavy as stone, and she could not breathe without pain. She looked back. She could not see the Taker. She lay down and closed her eyes until she could no longer feel her heart beating. She still held the ip by the tail.

Maug lay down on his back. He was panting, his arms spread out. Marwen watched his chest rise and fall and noticed how large his hands were. She sat up.

"Why does the Taker follow us?" he asked, rolling his head toward her.

Marwen frowned. Her breath was coming more easily now.

"Who am I to explain the ways of the Taker?"

"Can you feel her presence still?"

"No. She is gone." She was holding Cudgham-ip by the tail, glaring into his mobbleberry eyes. The tip of his red tongue was sticking out.

Maug stood up. "I will return for the pack," he said.

"No, please, don't. I am afraid," Marwen said, dropping the

ip into her apron pocket. She did not want to return to the place where Opalwing lay dead. Worse still was the thought of remaining alone.

Maug looked at her strangely and said, "I cannot see the Taker, but I can see these hills, that they grow no leaf or berry. Even ips can starve to death in a desert. Since the wingwand is dead, we must either carry the pack or the Taker herself on our backs, for we will soon starve."

Marwen looked around at the rolling hills, bald and brown and stretching into the horizon. It was as though they walked upon the back of some vast gold-furred monster that threatened to awaken and devour them.

"I will come with you," she said.

When they reached Opalwing lying dead, her wings spread softly on the sharp grass, Maug spat.

"By the Mother! You should chase that ip into the desert for this."

Marwen said nothing but watched as he shouldered the pack with ease.

"Better still, throw the thing."

"No," she said.

"Why not? The creatures can't run very fast. Toss it and be rid of it," he insisted.

Marwen felt her heart's blood drain. It was all different now, just the two of them alone in the desert, but she was still afraid of him.

"You forget that this is not an ordinary ip, Maug. It is Cudgham." She drew him from her pocket and watched as he batted the air with his stumpy legs but less energetically than before.

Maug snorted. "All right, then, say he's Cudgham—so what?" He gestured with his head confidingly, as if to keep it from Cudgham-ip. "Chuck him. Good riddance, right?"

"You don't understand, Maug. I need Cudgham-ip like you need me. He is the only witness to my tapestry, and by one witness it may be remade."

"But you don't have—" He broke off.

A slow realization made her eyes narrow.

"You just want me to get rid of him because then you will be stronger than I am."

Maug spat again and shook his head.

"And what should I do for a tapestry without you?" he said, but a shifting of his eyes told her she had guessed right.

"Do remember that," she said.

She set her face toward Kebblewok, and they began to walk.

She listened for the water as the grandfather stone had advised her and often found natural wells surfacing in the hollows. There they would drink and dig up the roots of stickstem and sleep uneasily, and always the Taker followed in her dreams.

The only creatures they saw were ips and insects and sometimes the track or spoor of a bisor beast. Wind after wind, through many cycles of winds, they walked. Their food ran out quickly, and along the way they discarded the remainder of their gear as even the slightest weight on their shoulders became a torture. Marwen left their things as gifts for the little gods of the wells, and so usually they found water. Sometimes she caught Maug looking at her, but always he would look away. He was not kind to her, but he was no longer cruel either. Their sufferings bound them. Spiny bloodpetal pierced their ragged shoes and filled their feet with slivers when they became tired and accidentally stepped on them. Their homemade shoes were soon rags, their ankles and calves were scraped and raw from brushing the thorns of ghostflower that proliferated on the dry slopes. But they kept the dawnmonth sun to their right and Marwen thought that, if she lived, she would make a song for this.

One day they saw a wingwand flying overhead. They screamed and jumped until they were sure they had been seen, and long before the rider landed, they recognized the red-legged markings of Peggypin and knew that it was Buffle Spicetrader.

Relief flooded Marwen's being like a warm bath. He must have escaped, being away on a journey to the market in Kebblewok. She ran toward him, waving and smiling, feeling terribly young, promising herself to be humble with the man. Maug, too, waved and called out.

But as she approached, Buffle's eyes grew wide with recognition. He made the sign to ward off evil and flew away. Maug did not seem surprised but said nothing.

Soon after that Marwen ceased to long for food. She found less and less water at wells along the way, certainly not enough to bathe her feet. She muttered weak little spells of healing on their bruised and bleeding feet that, although they did not close their wounds, at least prevented infection. But fatigue was her greatest burden. She did not sleep well, even when she found a bit of soft grass around a well upon which to lie. The Taker continued to appear in her dreams, waking her, forcing her on and on.

When they had lost all count of winds and days, and the sun had climbed noticeably higher in the east, and when they had become thin and brown, and when the songs would no longer allow themselves to be sung, then they saw the buildings of Kebblewok nestled in the lap of the hills like a child-god's play toys.

CHAPTER SEVEN

FRESHWIND, NUWIND, ESTWIND,
THREE WINDS FROM THE EAST.
NORWIND, CULLERWIND, WINDEVEN,
THREE WINDS OF THE BEAST.
WINDSIGH, WIXWIND, WYWIND,
THREE WINDS BLOW FOR SLEEP.
WINDSONG, YOXWIND, LOSTWIND,
A HALF DAY'S TIME TO KEEP.
—A VEAN CHILD'S NURSERY RHYME.

HUNGER AND thirst and weariness did not dampen their astonishment at the sights and smells of Kebblewok.

"I didn't know this many people existed in all Ve," Marwen said. Maug scowled and started irritably at every sound.

Stalls of merchandise lined the road, bright booths filled with woven baskets and wind clocks, cloth dolls and heavy woven greatrugs. Painted pots of clay and bundles of straw were stacked against the perspiring stone walls of buildings; the bleats and clucks of farm animals in reed-fenced corrals drowned out the merchants calling their wares; and the smell of breads and sauces and roasting meat floated like spirits into their faces. The cooks eyed them morosely.

"There must be people here from all the provinces," Marwen said, her voice full of awe. "There's a man with dark hair from

Verduma, and there's a woman from Vaphrodia."

A tall beautiful woman, with long silver hair like Marwen's own, walked by them. Marwen was instantly aware of what she herself must look like—her gray spidersilk and her long silver hair covered in the brown-gray dust of the hills, only her flushed cheeks and dry gleaming eyes betraying life.

She could never have dreamed in all her days in Marmawell the prosperity she now witnessed. Finely spun and intricately dyed textiles were held out to those who passed by but snatched back when Marwen and Maug passed. Metalcraft tools, wire and basins were piled in polished order. Leather goods, glassware and food stalls lined the streets, and overhead, wingwands filled the air like clouds of color.

They walked along the market streets, mostly unnoticed and ignored, until they came to a stall that was no more than a little section of tiered shelves, and on the shelves were rows of neat shoes, boots, and slippers. On the greatrug was a bucket of clear water from which a slight black-haired man ladled himself a drink.

"That smells so good," Marwen said.

The man looked up, glowering. His two front teeth were missing, and his beard was black and prickly except where it grew out of his many moles. Those hairs were white.

"That smell is leather and manure and hard-working people," he said with a heavy accent. He looked at her poor dress and turned back to his work.

"No, I mean the water," Marwen said, and she licked her sunburned lips. "It is singing to me, and I can smell it, also."

The man turned back to her, slowly. His black eyes flickered, but his face was still. He glanced at Maug, who rolled his eyes and made as if to walk away.

"You want a drink? There's plenty to drink."

Marwen took the ladle from him with both hands and drank noisily. He gave her more, and she drank again and then offered some to Maug. He frowned and took the water calmly, but his throat quivered as he drank.

"Enough," the man said. "You wait now, then have more later." He looked at Marwen closely and at her feet. "You come far. You have a mother? Father? This man is your husband?"

"Me? Married to her?" Maug asked. He snorted.

Marwen shook her head. "No, no husband, and my mother is dead." Marwen glared at Maug. "But here is my father." She pulled the ip from her pocket and dangled the reptile by the tail, shaking it at Maug. Maug's head jerked back and he stumbled.

"Ip! Pru brucht!" the man gasped. "What mean you by 'Here is my father?'"

"Yes, ip," she said with a grim smile. "Actually he is not my father. He is my stepfather." Then her smile faded, leaving dust lines along her nose and mouth.

The Shoemaker came closer to look at the creature. The ip hissed violently at the man, and Marwen pocketed it.

"How is it you are not poisoned by this pet?" he asked.

But Marwen didn't want to think or talk about the ip, knowing that, though the people often disbelieved the magic, they still feared sorcery.

"You make beautiful shoes," she said. "I have come over the hills without shoes."

"You want to buy shoes?"

"No," Marwen said, stepping back. Somewhere, someone was baking sugar tarts, and she lifted her head to smell them.

"You are hungry. You have money?" the man asked.

"No."

"You have something for trade?" Marwen did not answer.

The man looked at Maug. "Big boy, you can work?" The man's eyes fell on Maug's waist where his tapestry pouch should have been, and then his molehairs bristled. He turned back to his work with a quick shake of his head.

Marwen looked at Maug. He swallowed. There were likely few in such a large city who cared if a strange boy and girl starved before their eyes. The smell of hot buttersoaks struck her. The saliva in her mouth went thin as water.

"Please," she said, "I have a gift, in spells and charms." She remembered her vow that she would not sell her magic for shoes as Grondil had done. She could feel her cheeks flushing.

The man turned back to face her. He nodded slowly, thoughtfully, never taking his eyes from hers. "I believe yes," he said softly. "You smell my water, it sings to you. You have this ip for a pet. I think you have the gift, you are one of them. My name is Crob. Come, help, and I will give you food and shoes."

Curtly and without looking at them again, the man had Marwen and Maug help him empty his shelves into bags lined with slots into which the shoes fit. He gave Marwen the water bucket to carry. To Maug he gave the heaviest bags and gestured to them to follow him. She was afraid, following this odd-looking man into the heart of a city she did not know, and she glanced back often at Maug, taking a dark reassurance in his presence.

At one point he walked beside her. "Here, you take this," he said shrugging off one of the bags of shoes onto her shoulder. "It wasn't my idea to do this."

"You should be grateful," she hissed, watching the back of Crob's head. "He's right—you can't work without a tapestry."

"Shall I tell him what is in your tapestry pouch?" Maug asked quietly.

Marwen looked at him sideways and said nothing. Her back soon ached with the weight of the shoes and the water, but she clenched her jaw and did not complain. She was too engrossed in the city sights to complain.

Wealthy women shrouded in robes made from the wings of wingwands strolled the marketplace with easy haughty steps, their laughter rising like a slap to the impoverished who called their wares. Many of the poorest seemed to know Crob by name. One old woman who huddled before a neatly folded pile of blankets did not call but raised her empty hands to Crob as he passed, as though she held up her poverty as a thing of weight and substance.

"Blankets, good sir? Have need of fine woven blankets?" Her voice was tremulous, her fingers shook and Marwen recoiled, thinking of the Taker.

"No, Grandmother," Crob said, "not today. But say a prayer for old Crob," and he passed her a silver bit.

Marwen thought she saw the coin hover slightly above her palm before her fingers closed over it.

"You must be doing well with your beautiful shoes, Crob, to hire help," the old woman said.

"Politha, for one so blind, you see much," Crob said gruffly, but Marwen felt the gentle teasing in his voice.

Marwen saw that though her teeth were yellowed and her eyes blind, her smile was beautiful and full of wisdom. "Aye, I see your goodness," the old woman said. "How is the lad?"

"Not much longer, I think," Crob said, and he nodded at Marwen as if they shared some secret.

Marwen sensed something magical in the old woman and leaned down to pass her a ladleful of the cool water. She was reminded too well of the Taker to find her tongue and speak, but she managed to smile. The woman drank and passed the ladle back to Marwen.

"The Mother bless you, child," she said.

Crob, Marwen, and Maug walked on. The streets were full of beggars. For some, Crob had a kind word or a joke, for others a little money and for one small child, a pair of shoes.

Soon Marwen was not afraid of this peculiar man. The manner of his walk was steady and sure. His head was bent like a man of hard work and sober duty, but he trod the road lightly.

He led them through damp walled streets that were littered with eggshells, broken pots and soiled straw. When the market stalls dwindled away, the streets were quieter and more of the morningsun's slanting rays warmed the cobblestone. Then the gray stone buildings ended. Mud brick cottages with thatched roofs like those she had known in Marmawell clustered on the rising slope of the city. Marwen felt the weight of the walls lifted from her and was surprised to feel the coolness of lostwind on her face. Now she could hear the crying and laughter of little children, the banging of spoons on pots, and she could smell wingwand manure and washday soap. Marwen and Maug followed Crob willingly into his cottage.

It was small and sparse, and cluttered with the tools of his trade: sheets of drying leather, scarred worktables, nails, molds and spools of thick thread. Scraps of leather, material and bent nails were piled up in a thrifty heap beside a dusty hourglass on the mantle. But the floor was well-swept and laid with small rugs for sitting.

Crob served them thick soup and a slab of seedbread. Marwen ate greedily. When she was almost done, she reluctantly saved a small piece of meat for Cudgham.

Through the east window, Marwen could see the sun, pale

like a pink moon below a vast continent of cloud. It would rain today or tomorrow.

"So, I do not know your names," the man said when they finished eating.

"Marwen is my name and this is Maug. We are from Marmawell, a village to the south." She glanced at Maug who shook his head, and she knew she should not speak of the dragon. He had always been secretive, never telling anything that he didn't have to, but now he was sullen, his silence thick with deceit. He pulled his knife and the black bone from his pocket and began whittling.

"Ah, Marmawell, from which comes most precious herbs and spices: lapluv, greencup and teas fit for the king. The fame of this village reaches even to other provinces."

Marwen was pleased and thought to tell him that she and her mother had cast spells on the very kitchen gardens that had produced those spices.

"My mother grew a little shumple and browm," she said instead, remembering the Tenets on modesty and humility. Perhaps, she thought, had she practiced them more in Marmawell, Maug would not be looking at her so with his hard gray mirror eyes.

Crob was silent for a time. Then he arose, drew from a bag a pair of shoes and, kneeling, placed them before Marwen. He did not look at her.

They were made of fine soft rupi leather, pale blue, the same blue as the round skystone she had found, so long ago it seemed, and the tiny buckles were made of some metal that gleamed like a bit of gray lake under a cloud-laden sky.

Marwen stared. The only shoes she had ever owned had been braided from strips of old greatrug, rough and long-wearing.

The man looked up and into her eyes.

"I do not buy magic. This is a gift. For magic, I give gratitude and much honor."

Marwen did not smile. For the first time, she was getting what she had always thought a fitting price for her art: gratitude and honor. Now, however, it felt burdensome. She wondered what this gentleman could want from her, and a silent secret place inside her wondered if she had anything to give.

"I do not know what to do," she said.

"What says your tapestry?" Crob asked glancing at her tapestry pouch.

Marwen blushed fiercely and looked at Maug defiantly. He smiled and continued whittling the bone into shavings. Crob made an impatient gesture with his hand. His voice was urgent.

"You know what it is to thirst," he said to her. "I know of a lad, about your age, who thirsts unto death. If you will help me save him, there could be greater rewards for you than these shoes."

Marwen did not hear the words of reward. She saw only the man wiping his nose on his sleeve.

"What is it you want of me?" she asked.

"Have you skill with locks?"

Marwen shook her head. "How so, when only the very rich have them? But I know the language of rock and metal."

He nodded.

Marwen looked at this lump of a man who sat cross-legged before her. His dark hair was Verduman, she thought. All the tales she had ever heard of Verduma had been told her by Cudgham, and all the tales were full of blood and venom.

"Are you Verduman?" she asked.

Crob looked at her for a moment. "Half Verduman," he said,

searching her face. "I was born on the divide, the son of a Venutian woman and a Verduman soldier."

She had always listened to Cudgham, only half-believing, but
now she tried to recall the stories and the descriptions of the
Verdumans. They were a dark people, she remembered, long-
nosed and broad-shouldered, a people who loved to fight and
quarrel but who were famous for their bravery. Perhaps it was
because for generations the Vean King had made his home in
the province of Verduma, and from their mountain people, the
Clouddwellers, the king chose his army. She thought of her
father and her own Verduman blood.

"My mother was driven away by her people for love of my
father," said the Shoemaker, "and so when I was very young, I
went to live in Verduma at his house. There I lived in the mountains. But there, also, I had no people, and I was not allowed to
train in their army when I was grown. I ran away, back to Venutia and to Kebblewok, and found that in the cities the varied
peoples of Ve manage to live in peace. Here I was lost among
the throngs, my accent one of many, my dark hair nothing more
than an oddity if I kept my opinions to myself. My hands have
much cleverness, and I have made a living, but now it is time to
make a life."

Marwen looked at him in silence. He seemed to be filled with
a heavy longing.

He continued. "I tell you this so that you will understand my
partiality.

"Several days ago a lad came to Kebblewok, a well-bred lad, it
seemed, by his clothing and his mount. He came to the market
and stood in high places and warned of a dragon that is destroying many villages in this land." Marwen made to speak, but
Maug silenced her with a withering look and a shake of his head.

"For two cycles of winds, the people listened to him as they do a poet—with enjoyment but disbelief. He told them that the dragon sought the wizard and that his quest was also to seek the wizard and enlist his help in defeating the dragon."

Marwen placed crossed fingers on her lips. She had never heard anyone speak of the wizard openly except Grondil in her own home. It was considered offensive nonsense. Few believed in the wizard anymore. But Marwen had learned of the wizard in the old Songs and the ancient prayers. Her hands and feet tingled.

"Did anyone know of the wizard?" she asked.

Crob looked at her strangely for a moment and then laughed, as if he finally understood the joke.

Marwen laughed, too, uncomfortably.

"Come," he said. "Bathe feet and put on new shoes, and I show you 'death-in-a-cage.'"

Marwen forgot her fatigue and the pain in her feet when she put on the soft slippers. Maug, too, was given some shoes for his blistered swollen feet, and he went with them back into the city. She watched her feet as she walked behind Crob Shoemaker.

The more she marveled at the beautiful shoes, the more she doubted her ability to earn them. Since she had turned Cudgham into an ip, she didn't trust herself. Or perhaps it was that she did not trust the magic that seduced her and tormented her in turns, that seemed to abandon, afflict, or exalt her at will, and demanded submission to a law that was beyond her ability to live.

She looked down at Cudgham, asleep in her apron pocket. "Talent without mastery," Grondil would have said sadly to see it.

"Wake up, sleepyhead," Marwen said, nudging the ip gently with her finger. The ip rolled its bleary eyes, twitched its dusty tail and went back to sleep.

"What a stodgy old lizard," she said, but a moment later she rubbed the lizard's back thoughtfully. It was not dusty but dry and scaly, the rust stripes were fading with age. How long did an ip lizard live? However long it was, the man was aging as the lizard lived out its shorter lifespan. She thought about Cudgham's destiny and task, that likely she had put in danger her stepfather's ability to complete that task, and that she may be responsible for another person spending eternity in that bleak land of death where unfinished souls went. Grondil had told her of such a place. She thought of herself in that dark land.

Marwen remembered Grondil's words to her: "You speak of the magic as though it belonged to you and not you to it." How had she ever thought that the magic was hers to do with as she pleased, to revenge where she would, to reward where she deemed deserving?

They walked among the walled parts of the city. The stones were silent and stupid in even rows, "but not as stupid as I," she said evenly, running her fingers along the mortar lines. She knew now how the magic could be taken away from her or perverted to do evil. Perhaps she could never have been made to feel so small, if in her magic, she had not thought herself so big.

She glanced at Maug, thinking of the villagers and wishing she could speak with them again, tell them of her new understanding. She promised the back of Crob's bristly head that no matter what magic he would have her do, she would try and stay her right size.

Crob led them to a street lined with taverns and arenas for animal fighting, back among the gray stone buildings and littered cobblestones. Finally he stopped at a place where four roads led to a square and pointed to the wall directly across from them.

She could see what looked at first like a gaping tooth-barred mouth in the wall, the two tiny windows far above it like eyes. It was a horizontal space hollowed out of the wall, about the size of a large man, with metal bars enclosing it. Behind the bars, like a piece of meat about to be chewed, lay a young man.

Marwen stared transfixed for a moment and walked toward him.

He was a little older than herself perhaps, tall and dark-skinned, with gaunt cheeks and wide shoulders that seemed little more than bone and skin. He was very sick, covered in spittle, bruised by stick and stone, and his lips were cracked, as though he had had nothing to drink for days. Sores oozed on pressure points over his body from lack of movement. There was an old stench.

Crob's voice whispered beside her. "Here he will lay until he dies and then longer, until he is nothing but bones—a reminder to all of the finality of death and the reward of wizard seekers." He looked around quickly. "Round the corner is a tavern at which the guards spend much of their time." The boy woke from a half-sleep at the sound of the man's voice.

"Crob!" he said in a voice that sounded as if it had once been full and deep and strong. "You've come to see me die. There won't be much to see. I think I'll spoil their fun and die in my sleep."

"No lad, you shan't die," Crob answered quietly.

Crob looked around him, but no one seemed to be paying much attention in the busy square. From a window Marwen could hear the rhythmic shunts of a back-strap loom and, further away, two men quarreling.

"You place yourself in danger by coming too often," the boy said, panting at the exertion of speaking. He smiled at Marwen. His teeth looked white against his dark skin. "You have a beautiful daughter."

Marwen could feel the young man's eyes on her in front and

Maug's eyes on her in back. Her skin quivered, tense in a desire to throw her head back and smile, and in an equal desire to lower her head and shrink away.

"No, lad, she is not daughter," Crob said. "But I think the gods sent her to help you. This morning as I was at market selling my wares, my water barrel sang to me, as though it gathered rain. Methinks it is crying to me to take you drink. So I resolve to take you drink at day's end and guards be hanged. But instead the water finds me this girl who tells me she has magic. Her name is Marwen."

"Marwen," the boy said, "my name is Camlach."

At that moment Marwen did not feel pity for Camlach. He did not invite pity, and she herself had been struck with sticks and stones, had been spat upon. In that moment she remembered it differently, dispassionately. This young man caged and half-dead made her see with new eyes all those who hurt others. She glanced at the people milling about in the square and felt for them the deepest pity she had ever known. She looked at Maug. He seemed shorter, thinner, weaker.

The lock that secured the bars of Camlach's tomb was a padlock, the pins rusted, the hasps old and ill-fitting.

"Crob, you could rip this off with your bare hands," she said.

He shook his head and held out blistered palms to her. "I have tried." Suddenly he picked up a stick and pretended to poke at Camlach. "Aye, daughter," he said in a loud voice, his accent thickening, "and if ye sass me more, I shall marry ye off to one like as this."

A stocky man, helmeted and with a scabbard at his side, sauntered over with his chest pushed out.

"What, man, what can ye have to say that takes so long? No more potter and play, move along."

Crob pulled Marwen away. Maug was two steps ahead of them.

Most of the respected people of Ve sleep during wixwind and wywind, and so it was during these quiet winds that blow in gaps and gusts that Marwen and Crob walked again into the cobblestone streets and high gray walls to rescue Camlach. The morningmonth sun had risen just a little higher, reaching its soft rose-hued rays down to the cobblestone so that even the garbage seemed familiar and less odious. Maug had insisted on coming along. His constant presence made Marwen's skin feel achy.

"This will be dangerous. You should stay behind," she said trying to disguise the impatience in her voice.

"What, and let you out of my sight, to run off?" Maug sneered.

"Where would I go?"

"To the Oldest, without me."

Marwen said nothing to try and convince him, nothing to start an argument. Anything to prevent Maug from telling Crob that she hadn't a tapestry to validate her gift. For she would free that boy; in this there was no choosing.

She glanced down at Cudgham sleeping in her pocket. He had seen her tapestry. He had also said there was no magic in it, she reminded herself firmly.

The heavy walls of Kebblewok felt oppressive, and Marwen bent her head back to see the sky. Several wingwands soared above, and Marwen could see their shadows touch the towers and rooftops faintly. Even if the gods had not given her the magic, she had it still, and she felt it surging within her, filling her being, preparing her. She felt it like a strength, a powerful but invisible muscle that caused her head to lift, her spine to become erect. If she could not see her tapestry, she could live it.

The magic was in her tapestry, she knew it, and she vowed then, with hen bones and wingwand droppings underfoot, that when she had her tapestry remade, she would fit it. She wanted to run toward this lad, Camlach who died so nobly, whose quest was her own but who dared to say it before scores of people. True belief could never be secret.

This, she knew, was what the magic was for: not for shoes, not even for gratitude and honor but for this: to make right that which was wrong. But even as she thought this, she felt the magic tighten its arms around her, binding her, restricting her, owning her. Every knowledge bore a responsibility; it did not liberate her but exacted a price. She remembered the hourglass Grondil had sketched into the dirt floor, and her words: "The higher your powers, the narrower become your options to use them."

Ahead of her, Crob was sweating. Maug clenched his jaw so that the sides of his face throbbed. Few were in the streets, only a blind beggar and a soldier or two dozing on their feet.

When they arrived at 'death-in-a-cage,' Camlach was awake. No guards were within view, but Marwen could hear drunken laughter not far off. The fever in the lad made his face swollen and dry, and his eyes gleam. There were new purple bruises on his arms and chest, old ones had become yellow and brown, and an ugly gash to his temple oozed blood. He tried to smile when they came close, but he did not stir.

"Since you came, I have been afraid to sleep for fear it would be my last. Is it now that you will release me?"

"Now," Marwen said tenderly. She saw that he had hardly dared to hope.

"I'm not sure I can walk," he said.

"Maug and I will help you, lad," Crob said.

Maug had been standing apart, as if on lookout. He coughed softly and reluctantly came closer. "Hurry," he said, the sweat glistening in the furrows of his forehead.

Marwen looked past him to a wingwand soaring. The magic in her became peaceful, and she felt a cool serenity still her heart. In that moment she was utterly sure of her power.

She placed three fingers gently on the padlock. The lock had forgotten the language of its birth as rock and raw metal, and knew now only the language of a tool that has listened to the whispering out of a thousand souls.

"I am old, I am old," it told Marwen.

In the language of creation, Marwen told the lock how she could return it to its mother earth, and in the next moment, the padlock's rusted pins gave way and fell into her palm. She dropped the lock into her apron pocket; the ip hissed and rewound itself into a smaller ball. Marwen quietly swung the bars aside while Crob leaned in with his arms outstretched, and Maug stood nervously beside him ready to help, albeit grudgingly.

It took all their strength to help him out, for though Camlach was wasted and thin from many days of fasting, still he was lanky, taller by a head than Maug and Crob, and built in the shoulders like a man already. He leaned on them heavily, but Marwen had no wits to help them. The very air sang to her of danger. She thought she could hear footsteps.

"Where can we hide?" she whispered to Crob.

Then Crob and Maug, too, heard the footsteps and increased their pace. "There is no place to hide," Crob said with such a heavy accent that Marwen would not have been able to understand him had she not already known the answer.

"We shall have to leave him," Maug said.

"If the guards come near, show them your pet," Crob said to Marwen between clenched teeth. It was clear that the young man was becoming too heavy for them.

At that moment two voices rang out in rage, and Marwen knew that the empty maw meant to be Camlach's tomb had been discovered. Soon, she knew, their cries would be echoed in every street, and they would be safe nowhere.

"Faster!" Crob said.

Camlach threw his head back and groaned. "No, leave me here. I think my ankle is broken."

"Will we all die for one?" Maug snarled. His face was wet and gray.

"Not much farther, lad," Crob whispered to Camlach. He looked at Marwen desperately.

From every direction Marwen could hear booted feet running and angry calls, but the feeling of peace had fallen over her again like a soft cloak, and she realized she knew where she was in the maze of streets. She knew where she was and who, around the next corner, she would find.

"This way," she whispered to Crob, and then she ran ahead and around the corner. There, like a queen on a throne, sat the blind old blanket woman, Politha.

Marwen looked into the woman's calm unseeing eyes as she approached, breathless. "Grandmother, let your hands be blessed. Please answer me this question. Who wove these fine blankets?" she asked, but she knew the answer already.

"I wove them, child," she said.

Marwen bent on one knee and picked up the old woman's hands. The wrinkled skin felt like spidersilk over bone.

"And what else do you weave, Politha? Do you weave the tapestry, or am I mistaken?"

The woman's voice was still old when next she spoke, but there was a gravity in it. "You have strong magic, child. What need has driven you to seek the help of a crippled Oldwife?"

But Marwen had no need to answer, for Crob and Maug came round the corner with Camlach hunched half-conscious over their backs. Curses and cries of alarm from many guards rang from the rock walls. They were close.

"Politha," Crob said, panting, "will all your prayers help us now?"

The old woman took only a moment to understand much. She stood up achingly and opened her palms out to him as Marwen had seen her do before when Crob passed.

"Good Crob," she said, "this is the blanket you have bought with your generosity."

Marwen saw then that the open palms were not a sign of helplessness but that they appeared to bear weight, as though the air were heavy above them and the fingers held substance.

The woman stretched her hands out like a dancer and flung something at them that settled on them like the warmth of the sun as it emerges from behind a thick cloud.

"Come under my magical coverlet," she whispered.

Five guards rounded the corner the next moment, swords in their hands and rage in their mouths. But with scarcely more than a glance in Politha's direction, the guards passed by and, in a few moments, were out of sight.

CHAPTER EIGHT

IN THE BEGINNING OF TIME, THE MOTHER,
WANTING TO GIVE HER CHILDREN A GIFT,
CHOSE THE BRIGHTEST AND MOST PRECIOUS
OF HER TREASURES, AND GAVE THEM THE
ABILITY TO BELIEVE. —"THE CREATION SONG"
FROM *SONGS OF THE ONE MOTHER*

AS SOON as they arrived at Crob's home, Politha put Crob and Marwen to work making tea, poultices, and heating bricks. Maug did not offer to help but sat in a corner with his knife hacking at a block of hard-soap. Politha hovered over Camlach, weaving strong spells of healing and working them with her hands. For many winds Marwen watched and helped. When finally they straightened and left his side, the lad slept peacefully by the fire and the purple bruises around his face had already become less swollen and dark. Crob took his wares to market so as not to be asked after.

"We have done well, sister," Politha said to Marwen. The old woman's hands shook with fatigue.

"I am not a sister, yet," Marwen said, "but only apprenticed. You know spells of healing I have never heard before. Will you teach me?"

"What do you know, child?" Politha asked. She did not ask to see Marwen's tapestry as proof of her calling.

"The spells for good blood and teeth and sure vision. The hearthside Songs that relieve a child's pain or cool a fever."

Politha nodded. "Those are good, but they won't bring back the dying."

Marwen thought briefly of Sneda. Why had they worked for her then?

"Come," the old woman said laying her hand on Marwen's arm. "We'll see how you do." She sent Maug for water and began to teach Marwen a few of the more difficult spells for health, one for dissolving tumors and stones, one for healing broken bones, and another spell for fertility and conception. She taught her where to find in the *Songs of the One Mother* the spells for strong hearts and livers, and for problems of the bowel. "Still, in all things, the Mother decides," Politha reminded Marwen often. The spells came to Marwen easily, like a childhood language returning to memory. Before long, Marwen was rehearsing spells of her own making. Politha put her hand on Marwen's.

"Child, you are ready. Never have I felt the magic with an apprentice so strongly as I do with you. And surely you have proven yourself in this day's brave deed. If you are willing, I will name you Oldwife, and your apprenticeship will be over."

Marwen looked at Camlach sleeping and cocked her head. She had saved him, hadn't she. Finally she had done something great and good with her magic. She wrapped her arms around herself.

"But I have so much to learn," she said. "I have scarcely read a portion of the *Songs of the One Mother*."

"Tell me what you have learned since your apprenticeship began," Politha said.

Marwen was silent for a time, listening not to her mind but to her heart. She said, "I have learned that wanting the magic is not enough, that it is not even enough to believe in the magic. There is so much more than wanting.... There is serving and sacrificing ... and obeying.... And I am learning to be not as the shadows that swell and shrink with the light of the sun. I am learning to stand still in my belief."

She looked at Politha and thought that the old woman could see her with her blind eyes.

"There is much that you can learn in books," Politha said, "but life has taught you much and will teach you more, and it is dangerous for one with such power to be un-Named."

Politha waited until Crob and Maug had returned and Camlach had awakened to announce the Naming.

Maug shook his head at Marwen as she was led to the east end of the little house and bade to sit cross-legged with her hands before her, cup-shaped. She did not feel that she was deceiving Politha. It was right that she be Named, and the first thing she should do with her full powers should be to retransform Cudgham-ip and have him stand witness at her tapestry making. Then all would be right, and her Naming would be valid.

Politha placed her right hand over Marwen's cup-shaped ones and her left thumb on Marwen's lips, and began to sing the Naming. As she sang she lifted her right hand slowly. Within Marwen's hands appeared a flame of cool white fire that grew as Politha's hand lifted: the werelight. "This gift of fire I give you," Politha said in solemn tones, "to light your heart in times of sorrow, to be a beacon to you when you are unsure of how to honor your calling or which way the tapestry leads you." Marwen sat utterly still until the Naming was over.

Then Politha spoke to Marwen of love, knowledge, and

magic, and the beginnings of all things. Many mysteries did she speak to Marwen that night. She taught her the meaning of the title *Oldwife,* how her calling bound her to the Old One, companion and husband to the One Mother, whose name was so great as to be mostly unspoken. She taught her that the Old One, greatest of gods, trusted all with his gifts: law, form, and ritual. But the Mother gave her gifts only to the few: vision, perception, and creation. She spoke to Marwen of light and darkness and of truth and untruth. When she was done speaking, Marwen was weary with the weight of new knowledge, but she stood and looked around the house at Crob and Camlach, and smiled shyly. Camlach nodded and Crob beamed, and it seemed to Marwen that the fire chuckled and that the whole world must be glad of her Naming. Only Maug glowered in the corner.

"For this we must rob cupboard and barrel to celebrate," Crob said, and Politha rose to help. Marwen escaped to a corner of the house. She drew Cudgham-ip gently out of her apron pocket and set him before her. He began routing the dirt-packed floor for insects.

While the others set to the task of preparing a celebration feast, Marwen sat cross-legged, Cudgham-ip before her, her heart pounding with anticipation.

"So. I have had my Naming, Cudgham-ip, Stepfather. Now I will have the power to return you to your former shape so that you might stand witness for my tapestry making." She closed her eyes and placed a finger on the lizard. She took a deep breath.

"Tro mereth i sar plemen, col!" she whispered.

She did not open her eyes for a few moments. Under her finger she felt the lizard trying to move away from her. Again she whispered the words, more desperately. But the lizard moved slowly out from under the weight of her finger.

Though she ate with the others, for Marwen that night, the joy in her Naming had faded, and soon after she slept again.

When she awoke, the shutters had been closed against a stormy cullerwind, and Camlach was sitting propped up. He smiled at her.

"You were talking in your sleep," he said.

Marwen rubbed her eyes.

"What was I saying?" she asked. He looked much better. The bruises had faded to brown and yellow, and the swelling in his face had gone down.

"It sounded like a spell," he said. "I kept waiting to turn into something." He laughed quietly. He had picked up Maug's knife and hardsoap and was carving it. Marwen shivered.

"That's not funny," she said.

He cleared his throat and made an effort to frown. Marwen began unwinding her braid. Politha had given her a comb, and she was surprised as she combed it to find Camlach staring at her. She squirmed and turned away from him.

"I owe you more than I can ever repay," he said to her. Marwen shook her head and looked away. Where was Cudgham-ip? The room was silent but for Crob's gentle snoring and the wind. Maug, too, was sleeping. It was time they were on their way to the Oldest. Being Named had not given her the power to return Cudgham-ip to his human form, and the longer she waited, the more difficult it would be to do so.

"You look prettier even than you did on the other side of steel bars," he said after a time. "And with your hair down ..."

Marwen frowned. "Why do you say that? I am not pretty."

"Who told you that?" Camlach asked, smiling evenly. He carved the lump of hard white soap leisurely, almost feebly, while he spoke.

"My nose is too long," she answered. She felt foolish and awkward.

"Indeed," Camlach said with a sudden air of concern.

"It must be troublesome to have such a long nose—does it hang in your soup when you eat? Does it obstruct your vision? Why, everywhere you go, people must stop and stare and say, 'Look at the nose on that beautiful girl. Is it not remarkably long?'"

Marwen's expression of disbelief dissolved into laughter, and Camlach laughed, too. Though both his eyes were swollen, she could see the laughter in them.

"I think that under your bruises you are beautiful, too," she said. Instantly she regretted having said it, and she began rebraiding her hair fiercely.

Camlach's brows arched, but he didn't look away. Marwen felt an uncomfortable warmth in the room.

"Do you live in this city, Marwen?" Camlach asked. The quality of his voice had changed, but Marwen could not say how, only that it bewitched her.

She shook her head. "My father was Verduman. I am going to his house." She glanced at Maug sleeping. "Someday."

"You should sleep again," Politha said to Camlach then, "before Crob wakes and scolds me for being too lenient with you."

Camlach and Marwen looked over at the blind woman who was silently cutting thin slices of breakfast cheese as expertly as a seeing person. Marwen blushed, and she saw that Camlach, too, had forgotten that Politha listened to their talk.

She leaned forward and said more quietly, "Do you really seek the wizard?"

Camlach nodded soberly. "I was very close to finding him until I came to this cursed city."

Marwen placed her hand on her chest. "I, too, seek him, or I will as soon as I have done a thing."

"What thing?"

Marwen looked over at Maug who stirred in his sleep.

"Do you wish for some cheese?" Marwen said to Camlach more loudly. She scrambled to her feet and brought the platter to him.

"Thank you," he said, but instead of taking the cheese, he took her free hand, firmly, gently.

"Here," he said, his eyes upon her steadily. "This is for you, to say thank you for helping me." Into her hand he placed the soap carving, a replica of a wingwand in flight. Vividly Marwen saw Opalwing's white wings fanning her.

Camlach's hand lingered on hers. In his eyes was a questioning, a probing, as if he would see into her soul, and at that moment she was afraid. Not even Grondil had looked so deep.

She backed up a pace and stopped, feeling like a wild animal, cornered and wary of every sudden movement. She looked at the door as if she would flee and then back to Camlach. His face was kind.

"When you touched me, I felt fire," she whispered.

Camlach's eyes left her for only a brief moment to glance at Politha, but it was enough. Marwen saw the old woman raise her hand to her mouth and her blind eyes widen.

"Fire, Marwen?" Camlach said softly.

Marwen lowered her eyes, confused. "It was not unpleasant," she said.

Politha covered her face with her apron, then pulled it down and groped her way to Marwen.

"It is a sacred thing you are feeling," she said gently, but Marwen thought she turned a stern face to Camlach. "Like a wild wingwand, it must be tamed and bridled before it can serve us."

Marwen's stomach felt pleasantly uneasy, the way it did just before she made magic. She ran her fingers over the smooth white soap carving and wondered what magic there was in the hands that made it. "I have never before owned such a lovely thing," she said. "Thank you."

Camlach did not smile, but his voice was as soft as spellwork. "Let it remind you of a wild wingwand and of me."

Marwen gazed silently at Camlach for a moment and then nodded.

Into the pouch on her belt, in which most people carried their tapestries, Marwen placed the ornament, being careful to let no one see that it went to the very bottom. Now more than ever before, she longed to fill that pouch and hold her future safely in her own hands.

She did not see that Maug had awakened and that from his dark corner, his eyes were bright and cold.

CHAPTER NINE

"FARRELL, MOST BEAUTIFUL OF OLDWIVES,
THOU ART BECOME WISE."

"NAY, LORD, I AM OF ALL WOMEN MOST
UNKNOWING."

"AND AGAIN MORE WISE."

—"FARRELL'S DIALOGUE" FROM *SONGS OF THE
ONE MOTHER*

"WHEN ARE you going to ask Politha?" Maug whispered. Marwen was kneading flatpans for their journey, sprinkling puffs of heavy brown flour carelessly onto the dough. She wasn't very good at this and wished she'd paid more attention to Grondil's instructions in the kitchen.

"Politha?"

"About reweaving my tapestry. You promised that you'd ask the first Oldwife we came to." He stood beside her, slope-shouldered and sullen.

Marwen looked up furtively. "Shhh!"

"I'll tell them about you," Maug said. There was a nervous bitter edge to his voice, but he kept it low enough that no one else could hear.

Marwen gripped his forearm with a dry doughy hand.

"Maug, not here. Not Politha. Can you not wait until we reach the Oldest?"

He said nothing for a time, and Marwen began to knead the dough again without taking her eyes off him. They both listened to the sound of Crob's hammer against a boot heel. Finally Maug said, "The Oldest then. But remember, I'm not afraid of you."

Marwen struggled not to glare at him. She put the bread in the bake box over the fire and sat with the others. It had become dark with thunderclouds, and the wind began to batter cold at the windowboards. They would not leave until the storm was over. She looked around the room for Cudgham-ip, but she could not see him.

The fire tossed and popped as it burned rushweed braids, casting demon shadows that danced on sheets of leather curing on frames. The fire shadows danced on the knobs and points and blades of the cobbling tools. The east window remained shut against the worsening storm. Camlach spoke, and Crob, Maug, Marwen, and Politha listened intently.

"You cannot imagine the destruction," he said. "Entire villages burned to the ground, men and women and little children scorched and blistered and charred black, screaming until their throats are swollen shut, and they die. Those that survive have nothing to eat, for the grain is burnt to stubble. Ashes fall like snow on villages to the south, and the sun is hidden in smoke."

Camlach swallowed hard and closed his eyes. It had been only a few winds since his rescue, but the spells had brought much healing already. "Your words constrain me to believe," Crob said, and he shook his huge head in sorrow.

"Has this dragon a name?" Politha asked.

"Perdoneg," Camlach said.

Politha's gasp was not heard, for the wind howled at the windowsill in that moment and died away to a moan.

"Perdoneg?" Politha said in a half-whisper. "Are you sure?"

"It is the name he gives himself," Camlach said and then, looking at Politha soberly, he added, "If there is some knowledge that you have concerning this thing, please tell it for the sake of all Ve."

"I will tell what I know, lad," the blind woman said after a moment, "not for the sake of Ve but for the sake of magic. The story was passed down to me from my grandmother who made me memorize it carefully."

She rocked a little from side to side, and Marwen felt her invoke a story spell.

"In ancient times there were many dragons, and they roamed the world and had divers powers. But they were small dragons, and grown men with their wits about them could defend themselves against one. It was the vestige of these that I thought was in your land. In that day many wizards roamed the land, also, bringing peace and prosperity to the people of Ve. An Oldwife in that day could live her entire life without ever burying an unfulfilled tapestry.

"But the people were not happy. 'Why should we endure these dragons that torment us and even carry off our children?' they complained, and so the wizards began to destroy the dragons one by one. After a few generations, the population of the dragons had been substantially depleted, but the records also say that fewer and fewer men were born with the power. Then one day, in this long ago time, there was only one wizard to be found in all the land, though he was a great and powerful and good wizard." Marwen's legs were folded under her, but at this she sat up straight on her knees. "I know his name: Morda-

hon." Politha nodded, and Marwen snapped her fingers in satis-
faction. The old woman continued.

"It was thought by the people that all the dragons had been
destroyed, but they were mistaken. One day from across the
water came an immense creature that filled the sky when it flew,
eating wingwands whole and able to curl around an entire mountain to sleep. The creature had given itself a name: Perdoneg.

"Morda-hon was wise and realized that as all the light was
now in himself, so all the darkness was embodied in Perdoneg,
and to destroy one would be to destroy the other. Morda-hon
spoke to Perdoneg of this wisdom, and they conversed for many
days. But the nature of the darkness is to want to comprehend
and overcome the light, and finally Perdoneg laughed and said
he had come to destroy a wizard and his heir, and that he would
do so.

"Then ensued a great battle, and in the end Perdoneg was
imprisoned by Morda-hon in the land of the lost—that place
where come to dwell all those dead whose tapestries are unfulfilled. There Perdoneg became lord and master of unfinished
souls. It is said that many generations of wizards have lived since
then, descending in secrecy, for as belief in dragons disappeared,
so did belief in wizards."

Politha stopped speaking. The fire cast sharp shadows on the
faces of the four, and Marwen thought she could see them all
burning in dragon's breath. In the silence of fire and wind, the
old woman added, "It has been long since I have found the
courage, in this age of disbelief, to say such a thing, to speak of
the wizard. Perhaps I am wrong. Perhaps the magic truly fades
from Ve. The Songs tell of an age when the magic will be done
away with, when evil will have its chance to reign in Ve. Perhaps
that day is now come."

"The magic is not fading," Marwen said starting, as if awakening from a dream.

Politha chuckled. "I should have known better than to try and keep this one under a story spell." Crob grunted and bent over his work again.

"Grondil, my mother, interpreted the tapestry without error and wove both truth and prophecy with her threads," Marwen said. "Her spells graced the spice gardens, for which Marmawell is known, and brought safely into the world every child in the village. And you, Politha, who learned the art of weaving so well, you who wove a blanket of invisibility, can you say that there is no magic in those hands that see what your eyes do not?"

Politha smiled and nodded.

"The Oldwives of the smaller villages have not entirely lost their art, it is true. But did your mother not teach you, child, of the way it was in ancient times, when the Oldwives' spells were not restricted to kitchens and gardens and inkle looms, when an Oldwife could be granted the gift of the staff as was Farrell of Old. Ah, Marwen, once there was a time when the Oldwife of the village was not feared but loved and respected. You, Marwen— were the children kind to you, honoring you for your gift?"

For a moment Marwen feared that every taunt and cruel trick she had endured was revealed in some way to the others in the room, and that they, too, seeing her weakness and vulnerability, would despise her. She glanced at Maug. He looked steadily down at the floor. She felt the walls expand, and Camlach seemed far away.

"I thought not," Politha said gently. "In the cities, here in Kebblewok and in other places, only the devoted use the services of the Oldwives for anything other than the making of the tapestry for their children, and even the tapestry has become less sacred, a thing to speak of lightly, even to ignore. They do not teach their children to believe in the magic. The Oldwives have become midwives. True, the people do still make sacrifice to the One Mother, but it is holiday, not worship. Perhaps, perhaps the dragon will instruct us, will send us running to our tapestries...."

Quietly, tunelessly, into the silence, she began to sing, her old voice quavering and haunting:

Here let me sing a story of Drude
who stepped over lava hills
and swam the white water
to come to a land of dragon bones
half-earth death diagrams
in the red sands
that filled the empty canyons.
all the summersun days he dwelt
in the purple caves
and wandered the soft yellow rock
eating the roots of stickstem
drinking the white water
and worshipping the dragon bones
that peopled the empty canyons.
finally his wanderings ended
at the base of a black mountain
and there he saw a living serpent
blowing billows of steam into the air
and stretching its wings like vast scarlet sails
to fly exalted, solitary
over the empty canyons.
then Drude returned home
to draw dragons all his days

and when people shook their heads
he sang, "My heart is an empty canyon."

When she was done, Crob arose from his cobbler's bench and fed the fire with more rushweed braids, as if he were cold.

Cudgham-ip crawled from some damp corner of the cottage into Politha's lap. Everyone in the room became still. He lay there double-blinking in slow motion, first one eye, then the other, again and again hypnotically. Hesitantly the old woman touched the creature's leathery skin.

Crob jumped to grab her hand away, his accent heavy when he spoke. "Is good, is fine, Politha. Is pet, see, Marwen's pet, but—uh—don't touch."

"So there you are," Marwen said. She picked the lizard up by the tail where he dangled undignified. "I thought I had lost you," she said. Angered at the relief in her voice, she added in a half-whisper, "No loss."

"Now there is magic!" Camlach said, amazed.

Marwen shrugged one shoulder and dropped the ip into her apron pocket. She opened her mouth to tell them all about the remarkable spell she had done to transform a man into a lizard, but she closed her mouth again. She had not been able to reverse the spell. She looked about the room for some object with which to display her magic but could see nothing for the gathering smoke. She smiled.

"If the magic were fading, could a mere Oldwife do this?" Marwen said. She stretched her arms out, fingers extended. Slowly the smoke gathered like breeze-blown mist between her outstretched arms, its grayness acquiring a gritty texture, darker, heavier.

Marwen smiled to herself, partly in pride, partly in the pure joy of the magic. It was a mastery like no other, in which she tuned her spirit to see all other things in their spirit form and then commanded them to be as she willed, as a painter wills color, as a weaver wills thread, as a poet wills words. The smoke that had only a short time before spoken the language of growing rushweed gathered at her fingertips and allowed itself to be molded and formed into the shape of a large ip, its tongue leaping from its mouth like a lick of fire.

Marwen laughed quietly as she saw through the haze of her little trance the astonished faces of Maug and Crob. But then the laughter died to a hiccough, and her hands dropped to her sides.

Always before, a smoke sculpture had faded as quickly as it was made, leaving the watchers wondering if their eyes had tricked them. But this time it did not fade; it boiled and bubbled and was no longer an ip but a dragon, its tongue a flame. Tiny glowing embers that burst from the fire hovered in the dragon's head like eyes, and the eyes turned to Marwen and saw.

Marwen cried out, and her breath made the smoke wings lift. The wind outside beat on the house like the sound of great wings. The windowboard burst open, and the wind roared like fire and wailed like children in pain. Crob jumped up and pushed the windows closed.

"What is it?" Politha was saying. "What is the matter?"

Gritting his teeth, Camlach rolled on to his knees, thrust a fist into the smoke dragon. Shards of smoke roiled around the room a moment and then faded.

For a long time, the room was full of silence. The wind shook the loose windowboards, and the rain fell hard as hail into the thatched roof.

"I'm sorry—I don't know what happened," Marwen said. "It is a trick I have done since childhood." Marwen could still hear her heart. The embers had looked at her and had seen her.

"I have never seen anything so—so beautiful," Crob said. "I believe the rusty lock you removed to free Camlach was ready to break. But this ..."

"It is evil," Maug said standing up stiffly. "Her tricks have brought nothing but evil."

"Hush," Politha said. "A newly named Oldwife must get used to her new powers."

Camlach stood and faced Maug but said nothing. Maug sneered and sat down. Marwen had not intended to use her magic this way, with tricks and illusion, and in a way it had not even been her spell. There had been some other force at work, some power that had sensed her own and had touched and embellished and magnified it. It was not a force of good.

"I felt almost as if the eyes of the dragon could see me, as if it were seeking me," she said staring at the fire.

"I know what the dragon seeks," Camlach said. "He has sent messages by way of many a horrified survivor. He seeks the wizard, but all say he seeks in vain."

"Because there is no wizard." Crob said.

Maug said, "Aye."

Camlach glared at Maug. "So said my people of dragons."

Maug snorted, and then there was silence.

Crob left off his shoemaking and joined them by the fire, shivering. "If the wizard lives would he let his people die by this dragon? Only one thing to vanquish this great evil, and that is a well-placed arrow."

The wind buffeted against the house with a force like the beat of great wings and screamed in the doorjambs and the chimney.

Politha groped with her hand for Crob. "This storm ..." she whispered.

Everyone listened. Maug's head was bent back, staring up at

the ceiling. His mouth gaped open, his body tensed as if he were about to run. A brief white light blinked in the chinks of the walls and the heavens cracked and thundered from end to end. The shutters burst open again, and the wind swooped in with a roar.

"One Mother save us," Politha said. Maug leaped up. His knees were bent and his hands fisted and he looked wildly from the ceiling to Marwen and back again, his face flickering red and black in the firelight.

"It is not a storm but the dragon's firestorm," Maug said between gritted teeth. "I've heard it before."

Marwen breathed deeply. There was the smell of wet burning straw bricks and the cry of an infant on the wind.

Crob stood to close the shutters. The rain lashed at the sheets of leather and the wind blew the fire out. Crob stuck his head out the window.

"There is fire—in the town below," he cried.

"Perdoneg!" said Maug. "She's brought 'im. The witch brought 'im."

"Hold your tongue," Camlach said to Maug.

Marwen felt the ground roll beneath her. She clutched at Politha. The wind whined, then whipped into a wail. Politha's blind eyes shone white as the room was lit by another seam of lightning, but Marwen couldn't hear the thunder. Above the thunder came the crashing of a great voice on the wind, a voice like the sound of a mountain crumbling.

"Listen!" Camlach shouted. Marwen listened. All the hair on her arms stood on end. The great voice was almost as indiscernable as the rumble of rain and thunder, but as she listened she thought she heard the words, "Nimroth ... Nimroth ..."

Maug grimaced and put his hands over his ears.

Crob and Camlach raced out of doors. Marwen ran after them. From all the houses men were running, their eyes lifted to the low dark sky, their hands white around sword hilts and bows. In the walled city below, black clouds of smoke billowed in the rain. Marwen could see no fire.

"There!" Camlach shouted above the shriek of the wind. He pointed upward. There was a fierce joy in his voice. "There is a sight that will make all other dreams die: Perdoneg!" His arms dropped, and he stood smiling savagely up at the clouds, his chest heaving.

At first Marwen could see nothing but the clouds rolling and steaming over the gray hills. Then she saw flames streak like sunlight to the west, and a moment later she made out the black shadowed shape of a creature whose great wings sucked and beat at the wind, and caused the clouds to wheel.

"Nimroth …"

Camlach threw his arm around Marwen. She stopped looking at the clouds to look at him, but his eyes were fixed on the sky. "That is the wizard's name," he said. He laughed and gestured rudely to the sky. "I knew it already, Perdoneg. But he is not here!" His arm fell to his side, and the other arm dropped from around Marwen's shoulders, but still he looked up. "Nimroth is not here," he said.

Then the rain poured down in dense cold streams, and Marwen could scarcely see Camlach. The sky lightened faintly as they ran into the house, and norwind died away to windeven. Marwen did not look up. She knew the dragon was gone.

CHAPTER TEN

INTELLIGENCE IS THE STEM AND STALK UPON
WHICH AGENCY BLOOMS, THE BRILLIANT FLOW-
ER OF LIFE. —*THE TENETS OF THE TAPESTRY*

MAUG WAS hunkered on the floor before
the dying fire, Politha was stroking his
arm and whispering a spell of calming. Camlach pushed past
Maug, ignoring him. He pulled off his wet overshirt and began
coaxing the fire back to life.

"So. I was not wrong. I followed what I thought was the trail
of the wizard to Kebblewok, and if Perdoneg himself came here,
then the trail I followed is the right one."

"Camlach, tell me what you know of the wizard," Marwen
said. She knelt beside him on the hearth.

The wind was blowing less violently now, more plaintively,
and the rain was falling like a whispered song. Marwen waited
for Camlach to speak, listening to the wind in the chimney. She
did not repeat herself, she knew he had heard. She had waited all
her life for this, it seemed; she surely could wait these moments

more. She reminded herself that if nightmares could come true, so could dreams. When he did speak, there was a nobility in his voice that caused Marwen to see him as if for the first time.

"I went to the old people first. Many would not speak to me. But after some days, I learned from the elders of a man whose name is Nimroth"—Marwen watched his lips carefully as they formed the word—"or thus he called himself in the foothills of the Verduman mountains where he lived. Folk of the heights claim he was studious and spent much of his time alone in his books. They say he became expert in the history of the tapestry and its meaning. When he first came to dwell with the mountain people, he loved to sing and recite poetry, but as time went on, he hinted at finding dangerous things, and one day he disappeared. I think this man is the wizard."

Marwen thought nothing, said nothing. She could hear each drop of rain falling on the straw roof. She counted each drop of rain that fell through the chimney onto the fire, watched it sizzle and smoke. Finally she looked at Maug. His upper lip was drawn back, and his right eyelid drooped almost shut, and she was afraid of him.

If it were true ... but it could not be.

It could not be.

"But where is he?" Politha asked. "A wizard would know that you cannot run away from a dragon. Besides, he would have left an heir. It is, by legend, the most important task of the wizard."

Camlach nodded. "Yes. No wizard would die without leaving his heir. But perhaps the wizard is not dead. Or if he is, the heir is unknown. This we know—that the heir does not dwell in the Verduman mountains. And this was my quest, to find the wizard or his heir. I have followed his trail to Kebblewok, speaking to old ones, believers, people to whom he revealed himself, but I can go no farther. I intend now to return to Verduma to seek the wizard's house and find what help I can there. They say the dragon sleeps around a lonely house near the mountains and allows no one to enter. They even say it is a magical house that the dragon cannot destroy. Some have died trying to get into it. I believe it is the wizard's house."

"Then it is death to go there," Politha said.

"To idly stand by while the dragon kills and destroys—that is a living death," Camlach said staring into the fire. "No matter what my father says, I will go."

"But not for a great while, Camlach," Politha said. "Not until you are well again."

Camlach looked at Marwen and smiled. "I look a lot better than she does right now." His face sobered. "Are you all right?"

Marwen nodded. She stood and walked to the window. She opened it and breathed deeply, desperately, the new-washed wind.

Camlach turned back to the old woman.

"No, I feel stronger every minute, thanks to you, Politha, and your healing spells. I have money." He held up his jacket and, working open a small tear in the lining, showed a gold coin sewn inside, one of many. "If without dishonor I could ask one more favor of you, Crob, it would be to help me purchase a wing-wand. I would begin my journey at waking winds." Crob nodded and then knelt before Camlach.

"I have a favor to ask of you, also, my Prince," Crob answered. The wind stopped utterly just as he spoke so that the words fell into the silence like the rain. Marwen turned to see Camlach's back arch and his cheeks flame bright red. Politha held her apron to her face and bowed, and Maug slunk further back into the shadows. "How did you know, Crob?" Camlach asked.

"I'm sorry to reveal this your secret, Prince Camlach, but I think you can trust all here in my house. My father rose high in Verduman armies and served your father when king was a lad about your age. I was young then, but king, your father, was kind to me, and you are alike as two wingwand eggs. I hope the king is well."

Camlach nodded. His eyes were deep-shadowed in the fire-light.

"As well as he can be," he said, "with Perdoneg destroying the land."

"And your brother?"

Camlach grinned wryly and absently rubbed his ankle.

"My brother is busy fighting the dragon at the head of my father's army in the foothills near Rune-dar where the dragon often comes. When my father would not allow me to do battle, I insisted on seeking the wizard. My father is not a believer and thought it a fool's chase, but he allowed it if I went in disguise. But now you know my secret, and you ask for a favor. What favor is it that I could grant you?"

Crob lowered his head. "I weary of exile from the only home-land I have known. I long once more to see snow mountains and drink with the brave men of Verduma. My hands would make leatherworks for kings, princes, queens. I would go with you, Prince Camlach, and be your servant, if you will have me."

"To grant that favor would be to put me further in your debt, good Crob. I need a man of your wisdom and goodness at my side." He smiled at Marwen uncertainly.

"Perhaps ..." he hesitated, as if thinking how he might phrase his question. "Perhaps Marwen, you, too, might consider join-ing me. When I am around you, I feel closer to my dream. It must be that I feel your belief."

Marwen shut the windowboards carefully, slowly. She could no longer hear the wind and rain above the roaring in her ears. She stood for a moment, then turned and faced Camlach.

"Yes," she said.

Maug threw some fuel onto the fire roughly and glowing ash sprayed into the room. "She cannot," he said. His eyes were narrowed and his jaw clenched so tightly that the sinews in his neck protruded and the veins on his forehead swelled. Marwen sank back against the windowboards. The wind seeped in cold and wet on her back. Camlach was still. His eyes went back and forth between the two of them.

"But Maug, did you not hear what the dragon said?..." Marwen whispered.

"Silence!" he said. He looked at the fire. "She must go to the Oldest in Loobhan first."

Maug had only to tell them that she had no tapestry, and that she was an exile from her village, to ruin everything—everything.

"I cannot," she said.

Camlach turned his face toward her, away from the fire and into the shadows, ignoring Maug. Something in the way he held himself, as if keeping a great control over himself, something in the way he turned to her told her that he was truly a prince.

"What the dragon said was 'Nimroth,'" he said carefully. "Is there meaning for you in that name, Marwen?"

Time was spinning her into a spidersilk cocoon. She knew that if she did not speak now, its threads would completely surround her, and she would not have another chance to tell it. She took a deep breath, felt the blood drain into her feet.

"I will tell you something," she said. "The dragon is not in possession of his tapestry."

No one spoke. She gripped the windowsill and raised her head high. She looked Maug in the eye.

"Master Clayware never spoke an untrue word, even you will not deny it, Maug. The dragon's tapestry is in my father's house, if his house still stands."

Slowly Camlach stood up. Crob stood, too, and then Politha. Only Maug stayed close to the fire. He was playing with a hot coal, teasing it with the hearthspoon, blowing it bright red, letting it die, smiling grimly.

"That is a precious secret indeed," said Camlach. "What is your father's name, and where does he live?"

Marwen stared intently at the dying ember for a moment and then raised her head to look full into the Prince's eyes.

"I am told he was from Verduma, and that his name was..." She swallowed. Her hands were shaking.

Camlach's beaten face filled her vision.

"My father's name was Nimroth," she said.

As in the faceted eye of a wingwand she saw him, confusion and revelation breaking upon his face by turns, a hundred polished planes of Camlach, peering down at her, seeing into her heart; and then only one face and one emotion: relief.

She was shaking her head and saying, "No, no, do not think it, it cannot be...." even before he grasped her arms and cried aloud.

"By the Mother!" He looked around the room at the others and back to her. He held her as if she would vanish under his grasp. "By the Mother! It explains the strength of your gift at so young an age, and the spell you cast so unwittingly over my heart, and why you were led here.... If this house in Verduma, the one of which I spoke, if this were your father's house ... no wonder the dragon seems drawn to it. If it contains the dragon's tapestry ... Is your father alive or dead?"

Looking into his face, she could believe it. Almost. "I don't know. He never came for me," she said.

"In any case, you are the wizard's heir."

She felt her face crumple into a frown. "A wizard's heir would be so much greater than I."

"It is a fearful thing to become one's own god," Camlach said. He bent his knees so that he might look into her eyes. "It does not lower your god but raises you. What god wants her child forever to eat the dust before her eyes?" Then he laughed exultantly and lifted her in his arms.

"Enough!"

All eyes turned to Maug. The heavy hearthspoon was in his hand, and his hand twitched. Camlach let her down gently, but his hand gripped her arm.

"She? The wizard's heir? This skinny gray-faced girl who cheats her way into her Naming. You who call yourself a prince, look in her tapestry pouch. Look! It is empty. She is a soulless one, born with no tapestry. Could a soulless one be the wizard's heir?"

Camlach laughed shortly, unbelievingly, and then, looking at Marwen's face, became silent.

The silence in the room pressed in on Marwen's ears, pressed down on her head so heavily that she felt she must collapse under the weight of it. Even the wind died suddenly, and the tiny whisper of the hourglass stopped. Crob and Politha had bent their heads down, but Crob glanced up at her with huge pity in his eyes.

"No, not soulless. I am not soulless. My tapestry was burned," Marwen said, looking from face to face. Camlach's hands had dropped away from her arm, and where he had touched, her arm felt cold. "My stepfather burned it—that was when I turned him into an ip...."

"Liar," Maug said quietly. He took a stride toward her, raising the soot-smeared hearthspoon, and then he stopped.

Between him and Marwen was the ip, its tail stiff in a fighting stance, its red tongue flickering. It hissed at Maug, and he stepped back, ashen-faced.

There was another long heavy silence.

"That is no ordinary ip," Crob said finally, pointing.

"The girl is no ordinary Oldwife," Politha said. "If you have a witness, I will remake your tapestry, child."

Marwen almost cried out in pain at the disappointment in Politha's voice. She had deceived this kind old woman.

"My stepfather is the only witness, and I—I cannot reverse the spell. I have tried every spell in the Songbook. That is why I sought the Oldest, thinking she could help me."

Politha shook her head.

Marwen had not dared to look at Camlach. She could not bear to see his belief in her become suspicion.

"She has no tapestry to reweave. I have known her since we were children," Maug said to Politha. He looked at the hearth-spoon in his hand and set it down. "But you can remake my tapestry for me, that was burned by the dragon."

"And who will witness for you?" the old woman asked sharply.

"Marwen," Maug answered. He ran his fingers through his greasy hair and smoothed it.

"A soulless one?" Windeven had softened away to windsigh, and though the rain had almost stopped, the eaves still gurgled and dripped. Maug stared at the old blind woman who did not blink or seem to breathe. "No soulless one can witness a tapestry," she said firmly.

Maug ran his hand over his face. He looked blankly past Marwen. He had forgotten her. It was nothing to him that he had just made her a different person in the eyes of all these people—

not a wizard's heir, not even an Oldwife but something less than human, something that lived and breathed without a soul, something small and ridiculous and evil.

"Then we will go to Loobhan, to the Oldest, as we had planned," Maug said.

"No," Marwen said. The magic was surging through her now like a windstorm, a half-stifled rage. It gathered at her fingertips like webstuff. "You have nothing to hold me with now, Maug. I will go to my father's house ... with Camlach...."

But Crob and Politha turned away from her. She forced herself to look at Camlach. The hollows in his cheeks were gray, and his bruised eyes were black in the shadows.

"One without a tapestry should not die," he said. "And the name Nimroth is not unheard of in Verduma. Perhaps it is not much evidence."

Marwen folded her fingers into her palms, held her arms close against her sides. She was afraid to speak.

"Marwen," Politha said, "you have seen the dragon. Should you die before your tapestry is fulfilled, you will toil in his kingdom and do his bidding." Her words were careful, her voice purposely kind, and Marwen thought she heard an edge of loathing in it.

"The dragon's tapestry is mine," she said at last, shrilly. "You won't find it without me. I will hide it with spells. Even as I speak, I weave them." She spoke more and more quickly. "It is a valuable thing to know that the dragon is without his tapestry, and for that knowledge there will be a cost: a wingwand, a beast strong enough to carry us across the wilderness to Loobhan."

Maug shrank back into the shadows. The fire hissed and sputtered fitfully. Politha and Crob bent to unroll their greatrugs for the sleeping winds were nigh, but their movements were slow and sad.

"Agreed," Camlach said. His mouth sagged as if he remembered his bruises. Then, "Marwen—"

She didn't look at him. She looked at the hourglass. "Don't pity me," she said.

That night Marwen dreamed of a white wingwand burning, its body blackening in dragonfire, its wings melting like silk in the flames, burning until there was nothing left but an eye spinning in the ashes, and it was looking for her.

CHAPTER ELEVEN

THE ESSENCE OF MAGIC IS NOT SO MUCH IN
THE SPELL BUT IN THE WORDS THEMSELVES.
ANY MAN WHO SPEAKS TAKES A FORM OF
MAGIC IN HIS MOUTH. ANY MAN WHO WRITES
WORDS PLAYS WITH WIZARDRY. —*TENETS OF
THE TAPESTRY*

*T*HEY ALMOST left without her at the next waking wind. But she followed, her face set, her hands curled and stuffed into her apron pocket on either side of Cudgham-ip. Crob had protested when Camlach said he would choose his own mount, but he had been consoled that the city soldiers would be busy with the fire damage. They said nothing when she followed them, stomping proudly behind, Maug in tow like a pale shadow.

The streets were sodden and muddy with ash. The market was closed. Only the bones remained: old tables black with puddles, frame casings for hanging wares blown over, broken shelves and the refuse of the day before. Their footsteps echoed unevenly. They stepped over discarded fruit peels, bits of torn oilcloth and shards of broken clayware. On either side of her were the dull silent stone walls and before her the bent backs of Crob and

Camlach. Maug walked apart from them, but she did not look at him.

She could never have said what she felt at that moment. She thought of the Stumble, the brook that ran through the hills and into Marmawell, and how it looked when it was dry in drought, no more than a gash of mud and stone, and buried in the mud, the slimy eyeless creatures that slept, waiting for the water to return. Which was the brook: the wormy bed in which the water ran or the bright quick water that hastened after a spring rain, cool and clear and silvered with little fish? And who was she? A young Oldwife who could spin spells like threads, whose father was sought by dragons, or a sorceress, a girl without a tapestry, a girl who lied and deceived and brought black magic?

She bumped into Crob. They had stopped before a small, roped-off herd of wingwands bundled together morosely, limp and bedraggled as a bouquet of bruised flowers. They had been penned for a long time, and the stench made Marwen's eyes water. A near-naked boy standing by with a prodder approached them, winking and grinning.

"They're cheap today. Nobody buying today, see. Three gold discs is all—take yer pick." Crob stepped closer, but the boy barred his way with his prodder. "No closer please. They bite." He grinned, baring his brown teeth, and winked.

Crob growled, but Camlach shook his head, warning him silently not to make a scene. "That one, then," Crob said pointing to a handsome female with pale blue head, feet, and wings.

"Ah, Chalkhill Blue. Good choice, ol' molehead," the boy said. Crob growled again.

"I will have the young male with the hump," Camlach said quickly. He had chosen a huge orange and scarlet beast, and when its wings rustled, they flickered like flame. It appeared to be a muscular animal, though its backfur, even from here, looked dirty and matted.

"Wi-Bisti," the boy nodded.

"And one more," Camlach said. Marwen met his eyes. His eyelids were blue from bruising and his lip seemed drawn down by a scar on his mouth. He was much better. But even in the cage where she'd first seen him there hadn't been this much pain in his eyes. He didn't smile at her, but neither did he look away. "Your price was one wingwand. You can share your mount with Maug if you will."

Marwen nodded once and pointed into the herd. "I will have that one, the mottle-brown."

The naked boy shook his head. "That one don't have a name. Flew into the herd during the storm. Could be bad luck, but," he winked and grinned, "too late now." He led the three beasts they had chosen away from the rest of the herd and pocketed the money Camlach gave him. "The folks is as good as the people, now," he said, and he sauntered back to the herd, wielding his prodder like a cane.

The beasts were hungry. Their antennae drooped. Crob shook his head and ran his hand over the blistered hocks and hinds of his animal. He was sweating. "This one—I am not sure she can carry very fat me."

Camlach examined his animal is disgust, then looked up at the dirty lad. "I ought to teach you not to cheat your betters," he said.

"Who is better, scarface?" the boy said laughing, and then he stopped. His prodder fell to his side. "Say, don't that scarface look familiar?" In the next moment he was gone, running on bare silent feet.

"I don't like that lad. We should be swift," Crob said.

Marwen patted her wingwand. It was a docile creature, and, though its backfur had been fouled by the black greasy rain, it was by far the best of the three.

"Mothball is your name," she said.

"Look, she has never been clipped," Camlach said, reaching under Mothball's wing, but as he did so, his hand brushed Marwen's hand.

Marwen stood still. She did not look at Camlach. But the hand Camlach had touched trembled and from that one touch the blood rolled in her veins like some scalding magic.

Camlach, too, was still. "She may be a wild wingwand or one half-tamed that escaped," he said. "She may be hard to control."

Marwen said nothing.

"Were it not for your magic, Marwen, I would be dead," he said, moving closer. "Come to me when you have your tapestry."

"I will not come," she said.

His face was quiet, but his eyes were filled with the look of one who had wakened to find his dreams are not real.

"Come," he said again.

"If I have any pride I will not come," she said, but the blood-magic made her shake her head and smile. "So expect me."

"Guards!" hissed Crob.

Maug leaped onto Mothball.

"Ho! You! Halt!" A tangle of soldiers ran with heavy booted feet toward them. One of them was a guard that had watched over Camlach when he was entombed.

Marwen mounted the wingwand in front of Maug. Camlach was still watching her, smiling. "Watch, Prince," she said. "Watch how I fly this wild wingwand."

"Fly! Fly!" Crob called to Camlach, but the Prince was watching her. Mothball bucked once and then rose into the air, flying south and east.

Below her, Marwen could see the soldiers were almost upon Camlach, and his wingwand was slow in takeoff. Marwen whispered a spell into the wind, a spell for strength to his beast and Crob's. Then they, too, were airborne.

The rain had turned the brown muscled hills green.

The solid gray sky closed the world in like a vast empty skull, with low-floating cloud like bits of white matter still clinging to the bone. In the east a vein of bloodred sunlight oozed through on the horizon, and the wind blew, moaning and uneasy, like the ghosts of bad dreams.

Before, Marwen had always felt healing and happiness in the hills, and she had milked their magic into her being. But these hills withheld their power, as though they would force her back. When Mothball landed to eat near a spring, Marwen stayed close to the beast, feeding her flowers—fon and bugboots, and gall-pollen where she could find it. Maug hovered nearby like a shadow, silent, dark, and distorted, until she sent him away to look for more treats for Mothball. He disappeared over a hill, and Marwen filled her lungs with air.

"Such a sorry thing you are, Mothball," she said. "Eat, eat." Her words seemed muffled and her voice small on the far-stretching slopes. There was not another man or beast for as far as the eye could see, and Marwen had never felt so alone.

As Mothball grazed and Cudgham-ip harvested insects, Marwen rested on the hillside beside the spring. She thought of Camlach and that, if only she could believe it, he loved her. Her own love for him was emerging from her heart as a brilliantly-hued newborn wingwand emerges from its shell. She thought of

Grondil and ached for her council. She rolled onto her stomach and pressed her cheek against the earth. She stretched out her arms and grasped the earth with her hands, remembering the dragon like a great winged cloud, blacker than the storm clouds, moving across the sky and speaking her father's name.

"Oh, Mother," she whispered into the dust, "beautiful One Mother—the Oldwife Grondil told me that I was promised to you and to your children, the gods. But what am I that you should want me? Could it be that I am...?" She stopped, unable even to say the words. "I am small, Mother, and weak, and I am lost, knowing not the way I should go, nor what I should do, having no tapestry."

For a long time, Marwen lay very still, listening. She heard the pulse of the earth's heart far beneath her and remembered a time when she had wondered if it beat for her. Then her life had only one course. Now the future had become shrouded. It stretched before her, vast and pathless, every direction ending in fear and failure. Then she had dreamed of finding a wizard who did not exist; now she sought in reality a wizard who was afraid to face the dragon and who might, wonder of wonders, be her father. Then she had one passion—her magic; now there was also Camlach, he a prince and she, or so Camlach thought, a soulless one. Perhaps they were right, perhaps she had been without her tapestry so long that her soul had blown away on the wind, perhaps it was her soul that piped tunelessly in the folds of the hills. She listened, her eyes dry.

After a time she lifted her head. She had heard this lilting tuneless voice before. It was the clear water of the spring. Remembering the advice of the grandfather stone, she crawled to its edge and looked into its depths, and in a moment, bright and bold, beneath a quivering layer of water, appeared a three-dimensional world of mountains and sky and grass and flowers. Marwen cried out in wonder and reached down her hand to touch the little weedsheep that grazed on the mountainside, but her hand entering the water disturbed the picture, and it vanished in ripples.

"No, come back," she laughed, and when Cudgham-ip came close to the water to drink, she shooed him away. She stayed very still until the water was as clear as a mirror, and the little world was again beneath the surface of the spring.

There was a shack on the mountain slope. Flowers grew wild around the shack, in the windows and on the roof, and Marwen could see each tiny flower in exquisite detail. In a moment her eye was drawn elsewhere, for a party of wingwands came flying with great speed over the lower end of the slope. Riding the beasts were fighting men, the King's soldiers, Marwen thought, for their shields and cloaks bore the King's insignia. Almost all carried at least one passenger—village men, women, and children. The soldiers dismounted in a field of yellow flowers at the base of the hill and helped their riders down. Marwen saw that the people the soldiers helped were hurt and wounded. Her delight turned to horror. They had been burned. Marwen could see a mother whose hands were white as wax, the fingers mere stubs, holding and stroking and speaking softly to her child as it wailed in pain. She watched as a soldier spread a cloak over the hairless head of a girl about her own age who had died.

The tiny soldiers in the watery picture herded the group of peasants into the middle of a circle that the wingwands had formed. The soldiers drew their arrows as over the top of the mountain flew an enormous creature of august beauty. Its shape was lizardlike, its scales silver-black, reflecting the summersun into a thousand, thousand rainbows. Beneath the creature's diaphanous taloned wings, the mountain seemed shrunken and insignificant. "Perdoneg," Marwen whispered, and her breath ruffled the surface of the water. From the dragon's mouth came a curl of blue fire, and its eyes glowed and faded like burning embers as it looked on the huddled group below it.

Bravely the soldiers sent their arrows heavenward, but none pierced the dragon's thick scales, and after circling the mountain once more with two wingstrokes, the creature descended upon them and killed them all with one blast of its flaming smoking breath.

Marwen pulled back and screamed. She could not remove her eyes from the scene.

The dragon looked at her. As though the spring were a window into her world, Perdoneg looked at Marwen and saw her.

He began to fly toward her, as if he would come through the surface of the water.

"So it is you, Marwen," he hissed, and his voice was like the wind in a field of grass. "Daughter of Nimroth, heir to the wizard, come to me. You are mine."

On he came until the vision of him filled the entire spring, and Marwen, in terror, splashed the water violently to dispel the image.

"'Daughter of Nimroth, heir to the wizard, daughter of Nimroth, heir to the wizard, daughter of Nimroth...'" The words rolled over and over in her head until she thought she must scream to stop them.

She sat beside the dim weed-filled water for a long time, her body still and quiet, her mind racing, reeling with fear and with something else. There were no more images in the water, save the grim face of a girl she no longer knew. She was afraid, for Perdoneg knew her name and sought her, and his magic was great. So long as she had no tapestry, she did in truth belong to him.

Fear welled up in her like a filling blister, but the girl in the water smiled. For she was Marwen, Daughter of Nimroth, heir to the wizard.

"It is seemly that one so evil should believe the words of this creature from hell." It was Maug.

Marwen started, not understanding his words. He stood a few paces from her, his fists clenched, his eyes wild, but compared to the dragon, he was a child, a silly child having a tantrum.

"I have had a seeing...." she said, not really to him but to herself.

"I saw your 'seeing,' though by what power you brought it, I would not say," he growled.

She looked at him sharply.

"Was it not real? Was that not the dragon you saw with your own eyes?"

"It was," Maug said.

"Then it is true." She looked to the northwest where she knew was the province of Verduma. "I am the heir. He will come for me. Perdoneg will seek me now, and one cannot run away from a dragon."

She felt Maug's anger like a storm cloud, felt him come close. She looked back at him. His face contorted and a crack of laughter burst from his lungs as his hand cracked against her face.

Her cheek burned a moment and then felt cold, so cold she touched it to see if she were bleeding. Her skin was hot and dry.

"I have known you since we were children, Marwen. I know you. Better than Camlach knows you. You are nothing, no one." He poked her hard with his finger. "You are clumsy and doltish. If I believed you were the wizard's heir, then I would be even more the unbeliever." He laughed on and on until he could only moan and hold his stomach. Finally he said, "If you were ... the wizard's heir, what should you do? You have no staff and no skill to battle with dragons. How could you help your Prince Camlach? You are no one, a village Oldwife's adopted child, a refugee."

Marwen knelt before the spring. Slowly she raised in cupped hands the cool water to her face and splashed it on to her skin. It was the same cheek that Cudgham had struck. She washed her neck, arms, and legs, slowly, deliberately. Then she waited for the spring's surface to become still, until her reflection was clear as a mirror. She teetered on the brink of belief, between two truths. Sometimes, or perhaps always, it was the knowledge of one's tapestry, not the fact, that made it true. The tapestry was not the thief of agency, it did not rob her of making her own life: it was a guide, a map to a place that was already within her heart.

He sees the world from his own eyes, she thought, and he sees a world of ugliness. There is no spell to change that.

"I am not ugly," she said, and in her voice was belief and utter calm.

Maug and Marwen stared at each other. Nuwind blew his brass-colored hair across his eyes, and he blinked.

"We will leave now for Loobhan, for the Oldest," he said. The laughter was gone from his voice.

She put her cool hand on her cheek.

It would be easy to do as he asked, to run away from the dragon, perhaps, with the help of the Oldest, to reverse the spell on Cudgham-ip and obtain her own tapestry. Then she would be safe. Then she would have her way made plain, her way through life and her way to the lands of the dead. But how strange, to leave behind living to obtain a map for her life. Already sorrow and good sense had taught her that in her tapestry would be a white wingwand, moons for femininity, and perhaps ... a crown. And living would teach her more, as Politha had promised.

She peered into the depths of the spring. She could see only the blackness of deep water. But no, there was a shape around the blackness. It was the shape of a head, roundish like a child's, but the skin was charred to a perfect blackness.

"The dragon will find me if I run away," she said. "But he will not expect me to seek him. I am going to Verduma, to my father's house."

"To your Verduman Prince, no doubt, and to your death. Well, I will not go."

She felt his hatred reaching out long white fingers toward her, but when they touched her, she felt something else less clean than hatred.

She said, "You must come. I must make haste, so I need Mothball."

"I will not go."

"Then I must leave you here in the hills, and Loobhan is many days' journey yet." She gathered Cudgham-ip into her apron pocket. As she straightened, Maug threw his arms around her to bind her. She struggled to breathe against the press of his arms.

"Leave me, and I will live to hate you," he whispered into her ear. "I will drink of my loathing for you and eat of my revulsion every step of my way across these hills. And if I die, I will die cursing you."

"Maug, I'll come back," she said struggling. "I'll stand witness for your tapestry.... I promise...."

"You will die. Nothing can stand against the Serpent."

His fingers dug into her breast. She closed her eyes and saw the white fingers in the places of magic inside her, and she saw herself peeling them back and back....

There was a snapping sound, and Maug fell away with a yelp. He squirmed on the ground until she went to him and with a word healed his broken finger.

"Come with me," she made herself say.

He did not answer, only looked at her with eyes she could not understand, white eyes.

Marwen hesitated and then took her tapestry pouch from around her waist. She put the wingwand ornament that Camlach had carved for her into her apron pocket along with Cudgham-ip and gathered some rocks to put in the tapestry pouch. She whispered a spell over them and watched as they glowed red-hot, then handed them to Maug.

"With this you can roast roots and leaves to make them edible." She turned to Mothball and removed the stockings from her antennae. "Come, let us fly."

She dropped the old rusted lock near the spring as they rose into the air, and then Marwen set her face northward, toward Verduma. She felt the white fingers become longer, and then there were arms and wings, but they could not pull her back.

Chapter Twelve

TAKER POEM

HITE! LITHER! DOLLORUM DELLO,
THE TAKER'S FEET ARE SHOD IN YELLOW
WISS! MORAH! DOLLORUM DEEN,
HER BODY'S SHROUD IN GRASSY GREEN
TOOD! NIMMEL! DOLLORUM DU,
THE TAKER'S BIB IS BRIGHT AND BLUE
RUUT! PANLO! DOLLORUM DAY,
THE TAKER'S EYES ARE DIM AND GRAY
—A VEAN CHILD'S NURSERY RHYME

S HE COULD feel the searchings of Perdoneg over her head like a tangible roof, a hard sky alive with eyes and ears, hunting but too far away. He looked too far, unaware that she flew toward him. Like a chant, in rhythm to the beat of Mothball's wings in the heavy hot air of midsummer sun, she murmured spells of concealment and hiding. She did not venture near the cities and avoided springs and rivers whenever she could. Her eyes became dull with searching the bright empty sky for dragonfire, and though once she saw black smoke blooming like a bitter flower in the distance, she did not see the dragon with her own eyes. Always he pulled at her with his mind, called to her but from too far away.

The hills were not kind to Marwen, for they hid their springs, and there was little food to forage. Only Cudgham-ip grew fat, for though Marwen's supplies ran out quickly, she was careful to feed him.

She crossed the northern bay and entered Verduma further up the coast, avoiding the border cities. When finally she landed on the lush Verduman coast, she had eaten almost nothing for many winds, but she felt safe. She felt lost. Perdoneg had lost her and did not suspect that she would fly to his hill where he slept between foragings like a great black worm.

There was a weatherworn shack near the beach where she had landed, and for a moment she thought it was the shack she had seen in the spring. Flowers grew thick around the salt-bleached boards of the house and spilled out of window baskets and grew in ledges along the roof. The sweet-pepper smell of grasses and flowers filled the salt air. But it was not the same shack she had seen in the spring. She thought she might beg for a little bread there or perhaps buy some for the favor of sharpening a knife or two, but first she must bathe. Under the noonmonth sun Marwen swam in the sea until her fingertips and toes were wrinkled. By then her hunger was keen enough to give her courage to knock at the east window of the shack. She could see the shadow of a bed and a chair, and a bake-box was blackening over the fire.

A little face appeared, peeping above the sill, a girl with flowers braided into her hair. In a moment a larger and thinner version of the child's face came to the window, her mother.

"What pretty hair she has, momma," the little girl said. The woman put her hands on her daughter's shoulders and said nothing.

"Please," Marwen said, "I have had little but stickstem roots to eat for days. Have you any bread for a traveler?"

"We are poor," she said simply. "My husband is sick." The woman began to turn away.

Marwen put her hand on the windowsill.

"I have some gift with healing, perhaps I could help."

The woman pushed the little girl away gently with a whispered word and faced Marwen.

"Are you from Venutia?" the woman asked.

Marwen nodded. "But my father was Verduman."

"Come in," the woman said.

When Marwen's eyes adjusted to the dimness, she could see, beneath the blankets on the bed, a tall man with black hair, beard, and moustache. He was thin and had an old goiter on his neck, but Marwen could smell no sickness on him.

"She says she's a healer," the woman said to her husband.

Marwen sat on a stool at the man's bedside. The little girl came up behind her and fondled Marwen's hip-length braid until her mother drew her away.

"You bring no tools or medicine," he said. His voice was strong and full.

"I bring only my magic," Marwen said. She sat very still, her hands folded as is seemly for the Oldwife.

"Don't believe in magic," he said gruffly.

"Have you no Oldwife nearby? Who did the tapestry for your child?"

"The woman sent for one by way of her sister when her time came. Stuff. That's what I say—stuff. No such thing as magic."

He leaned toward Marwen in a confidential manner. "I hear that up north is a dragon who wants to do battle with the ol' wizard, but the wizard won't show. Now, maybe the dragon has magic."

He chuckled and drew the covers up under his chin.

Marwen recited silently to herself from the *Tenets* on anger. She kept her back straight and her hands still.

"What is the nature of your illness?" she asked quietly.

"Tired," he said. "Always so tired. Can't walk. The Oldwife that did for my wife, she gave me some herbs. Only made me tireder. Magic, huh! Stuff."

Marwen was having difficulty remembering the words of the Tenets. She knew she could cast no spell in the face of such doubt, and her stomach was growling. "Your wife and child are hungry," she said tersely, and then she took a deep breath. "But you must be hungry, too." From her apron pocket she drew out a smallish stickstem root, warm from being next to Cudgham-ip who yawned as she took it out. She placed it in front of the man.

"What do you dream of, man?" she said. "Do you dream of roast podhen, pollberry pie, hot grainbread?" The stickstem root assumed the appearance, weight, and smell of each food as she spoke it.

The man reached out and tentatively touched the bread before it resumed its true identity as a root.

"It's warm," he said, and his voice was full of wonder. "Woman!" he said, calling to his wife, "are you not baking grainbread with the last of the barrel?"

"Aye," she said.

He smiled broadly. "'Tis a quick and tricky hand you've got there, but 'tis no magic."

Sure enough, she could now smell the bread baking. She was faint from hunger.

"Come here, child," Marwen said to the little girl. "Do you have a doll?" The little girl shook her head. Marwen held up the stickstem root.

"This is a toy you might like. Shake it!"

The little girl shook the root and a musical tune played, an ancient tune to which long ago someone had put words about the Taker.

Marwen squirmed uncomfortably at the sound, for which tune the root should play, she had not chosen.

The man's face showed delight and amazement.

"Give it to me, child," he said holding out his hairy clublike hand.

The child ran to the other side of the little house and huddled under the table. The man roared and threw back his covers. He chased the girl around the room until, slipping under his reaching arms, the child hid behind Marwen.

"Mine, mine," the little girl whimpered.

Before Marwen could stop him, the man crossed the room in two strides and grabbed the root. He shook it, and again the little tune played. He danced a little jig and sang: "Hite! Lither! Dollorum dello, the Taker's feet are shod in yellow."

"Stop," Marwen said. He stopped, and she put her arm around the child who was caressing her braid again and pulling on her spidersilk sheath.

"Now do you believe my magic?" Marwen said to the man. "You're not so tired now. I seem to have healed you."

The man's wife bent and drew from the oven a large loaf of grainbread.

"The bread is ready. You would honor us in sharing some," she said softly. "No gifted one need beg bread in my home."

Marwen smiled at the woman. But just as Marwen rose, the child screamed a single clear note of pain and terror.

She looked down to see the child taking her hand out of her apron pocket in which the ip slept. On her hand were two round drops of red blood.

"Oh, Mother," Marwen whispered. "Oh, Mother, help." She gathered the child in her arms and laid her on the bed.

"What is it?" the woman asked.

Marwen searched her mind for every relevant spell. She spoke them as rapidly as she could—spells for healing, for magic, for growth, for strength. Already the child's eyes were glazing, and her flesh was hot. Desperately she thought, and desperately she invoked the spells, but something was distracting her.

"Stop that music!" she screamed, whirling round on the man.

He stood there, stupidly, and Marwen saw that he was not shaking the charmed stickstem root, but that it played on its own.

In the doorway, framed in an aura of light, stood the Taker, smiling and muttering to herself, her head bobbing beneath her hunched back.

Marwen hissed at her. The Taker looked in Marwen's direction and smiled. She reached her hands out to Marwen as if she would give her something. The man and the woman stood frozen in place, looking around the room. They could see no one. Marwen watched as the Taker turned from herself toward the little girl. A coldness filled her bowels. She had robbed the Taker before. She would do it again.

The little girl's father was still standing in the middle of the room staring at Marwen first and then at his daughter on the bed. Of course he could not see the Taker who came up behind him. With a simple spell, Marwen could send him reeling backward into the old woman's arms and The Taker would have her life, though a worthless one.

Marwen shuddered a convulsive shake that caused her shoulders to heave and her head to snap.

Her fear had made her consider the ultimate faithlessness—that of ending the life of another. That was the Mother's place and the Taker's task, and Marwen's hideous presumption made her reel with shame. Saving Sneda's life and thereby forfeiting

Grondil's, had been a terrible mistake. To send this man into the arms of the Taker would be sorcery, black art.

Marwen lifted the sick child in her arms as the Taker made her way around the man.

"Is it not true that the Taker must obey the wizard? Then begone old woman," she said, though her voice shook and was shrill. If she were the wizard's heir, the Taker did not obey her. She moved toward Marwen and the girl. The old woman's cataract-covered eyes wept, and the tears fell past her sky-blue apron like rain on a sunny day.

"Can't you wait? Wouldn't you sooner meet me over the body of a dragon, Mistress Taker? Or do you hunger for the dead he gives you?"

Instinctively Marwen pressed her back against the wall. She felt the breath go out of her. The Taker was close now.

"Will I see Grondil?" she whispered. "Will it hurt?" The child was heavy and hot in her arms. Marwen closed her eyes. A breath of cullerwind blew in at the window, knocking some pots to the ground with a clangor. A column of dust sprang up between Marwen and the Taker, but the dust did not settle. It roiled and grew darker until the Taker was eclipsed from Marwen's sight and only a lightless cloud was before her, around her, cold and thin as a void.

The opaqueness began to assume a shape then, the blurred outline of a man in robes, a muted arm, an unfocused hand. In the hand a staff, a softly luminous line that was visible enough for Marwen to see the runes etched along its curved top spelling one word: *Nimroth*.

The darkness that engulfed Marwen began to disappear like dust settling. The shadowman reached his arms around the Taker to embrace her. And in a moment they were both gone.

Astonishment and fear were in the faces of the husband and wife, for all they had seen was Marwen, pressed in terror against the wall, the convulsing child held in her arms, while her face grew pale and then ashen-colored, while she railed at the Taker.

The child moaned in her arms. Marwen watched as the color returned to her cheeks.

For the next three winds, Marwen nursed the child with spells of healing, powerful ones that she had learned from Politha when nursing Camlach. And with every third spell, she wove with word and hand a spell of concealment from the dragon, wove a web of clouding, forgetting, hiding. The child's mother hovered nearby, quietly fetching things for Marwen as she needed them. When at last the child slept, the woman touched her arm in gratitude. Marwen said nothing. Her head swam with spells and seeings. She glanced nervously at the ceiling and gathered herself to go.

"I heard you when you spoke of the dragon," the woman ventured. "I have heard that the dragon sleeps round a hill to the north and east of here, between the villages of Rute and Rune-dar. There is an Oldwife there who they say is very wise. Perhaps she could help you."

Cudgham-ip tried to crawl out of her pocket, but she pushed him back. She struggled to regain her wits and her manners. "Thank you," she said. "What is your name?"

"Sharva," the woman said.

Marwen stood and took her hands. "Your daughter will live and will probably have an immunity to ip poison. But for your quiet soul, there is a reward. May these hands grow the most beautiful flowers in all Ve, and may the wealthiest women seek you out for them."

"You read my heart," Sharva said. "But you have not yet eaten."

Marwen, walking toward the door, said, "No, I'm not hungry anymore. Goodbye Sharva, and the gods be with you."

"Goodbye, Marwen Oldwife."

Marwen looked at the man. Just as she walked out the door, he snapped the stickstem root in half and stared into the broken halves, mumbling to himself.

"Stuff," she thought she heard him say.

Chapter Thirteen

WHEN LIGHT WAS PUT THROUGH THE PRISM OF
MATTER, IT BECAME MANY THINGS: SPIRIT,
LOVE, KNOWLEDGE ... —"THE CREATION SONG"
FROM *SONGS OF THE ONE MOTHER*

*T*HE WIND was wild, the whole earth was breathing deeply, laughing and panting and singing, and the grasses, like earthfur, bent beneath the wind's caress. Up sprang the little wind babies: stinging thinwings, flying iyos and far-jumping jimmies, all doing their braidy dance with unseen curls of air. The clouds had furled into fans of white mist, and beyond them the sky was deep and wide. Marwen let her heart and her wingwand soar into them.

"Father," she said aloud into the wind, for the first time believing it was true. She had always believed in the wizard, but now she no longer needed to believe, for she knew. And she also knew that the wizard Nimroth was not afraid of Perdoneg, for no one returns from the land of the dead, not even to do battle with dragons. But beyond this there was a deeper joy within her: Nimroth loved her, and he had come for her. She wished she

137

could shout it to the world, to Maug. But Maug was too far away, and the world was too far below.

"Father," she said aloud again.

CHAPTER FOURTEEN

EVIL HAS ITS OWN KINGDOM WHERE A DIFFER-
ENT PENNY IS GIVEN IN REWARD. *—TENETS OF
THE TAPESTRY*

CAMPS OF refugees had sprung up in the hills and valleys, ragged groups of men, women, and children who hovered around pale fires, their eyes and hands dragged down by dreams and fear, victims of the dragon's violence. Among them, when she stopped to beg a little of their watery stew and hard bread, she first heard the rumors of the return of the wizard's heir. They warmed their hearts and hands over this hope as over a fire, and Marwen listened to them embarrassed, fearful, silent.

Marwen's hair color alarmed many people, and she avoided them when she could, until she began to dream of warm bread and fresh cheese, soft blankets and hot baths. Then she would tell them her name, Marwen Oldwife, and she would be directed to the Oldwife of the community. There Marwen was sometimes able to obtain food and a place to rest in exchange for assistance

in the tapestry making or in the soup making. Marwen enter-
tained the Verduman Oldwives with Venutian tales of magic,
but she made no spells but for the spells of hiding. The Oldwives themselves were almost as skeptical as their people. They
viewed the tapestries they created with an even temper, never
amazed or disappointed because they did not believe in their
truth. Once Marwen saw the tapestry judged at a death with
much wresting of interpretation, and with a limited and earthly
understanding of the symbols. But the further north and inland
Marwen traveled, and the closer she came to Perdoneg, the less
cynical the Oldwives became. At last, one day Marwen arrived
on the outskirts of Rute, a land of long gulches and hollows and
thick grazing grasses. Mothball was growing sleek, but Cudgham-ip was sleepier than ever, and his scaly skin hung on him,
wrinkled and old. She eyed wearily dark storm clouds to the
north. Asking at the east window of the first house for the Oldwife, Marwen heard a voice call out, "I am she. Have you not
been taught the summoning?"

"Oldwife of Rute, let your hands be blessed," Marwen said
smiling to herself. "A sister desires rest and repast if it is in your
power to give."

As she spoke, a woman emerged from the shadows. She was
probably about ten suns older than Marwen, but she, too, wore
the knee-length braid of a virgin. Her hair and eyes were black as
winterdark, her skin a warm dark brown.

"You are a sister?" the girl said. "Let me see your tapestry."
She did not mean the whole tapestry, she meant only the corner
in which was inscribed the calling. Marwen thought this through
rationally, calmly, while her stomach squeezed into a tight
painful ball.

"This is the first time I have been asked while traveling in your land these many days," Marwen said, and she tried to smile. It felt more like a grimace.

"Well, but I am a true believer," the dark woman said, "and these are evil times." Her accent was lilting, making each word sound new in Marwen's ears.

"I, also, am a believer," Marwen said, "but I have no tapestry." She could not believe she had uttered those words, and she listened carefully to the silence into which they fell.

The dark woman's face did not change.

After a moment Marwen felt she could not bear the silence, that she must fill it up with words and explanations and excuses. The wind pushed at her back. She felt her face twist a little, and she cleared her voice so that it might sound sensible and mature.

But before she could open her mouth to speak, the woman held up her hand, her palm, toward Marwen.

"I see that your story is a painful one, one that should not be traded for food and rest or even for compassion. Come in, and if we can be friends, I will share your burden."

The woman's name was Vijocka. She moved and walked with long graceful movements, taming the fire, quieting with a spoon a pot of bubbling mudbeans. Her demeanor was both queenly and plain, her speech was gracious and yet as familiar as family. She did not smile easily, and yet her laughter was quick and strong. She was large-breasted and tall, handsome. Marwen could sense her good strong magic.

Her home was sparsely furnished with a greatrug, pillows, and a clay table, but everywhere Vijocka had planted flowers in the broken shells of wingwand eggs: blue onion and liferoad, untamable mopple and soft brown leaflullen bloomed in the nooks and crannies.

She served Marwen fruit, beans, and porridge, then left to

feed Mothball, while Marwen ate. When she returned, estwind was blowing dry and cool through the east window and with it came the scent of fresh-cut brome grass, as though a large wing-wand herd grazed nearby.

"Do you have wingwands?" Marwen asked.

"I make a place for them to mate and lay eggs," she said. "I do not own them, though when I am in need, they will often take me where I must go. I suspect by your accent that you have come a long way, and your beast tells me she is very tired. Why have you come so far?" She poured Marwen a bowl of tea.

"You can speak with the beasts?" Marwen asked timidly.

"They allow themselves to be understood by me," the woman answered.

There was silence in the room for a time. Marwen listened to the wind. She shivered. Was it speaking her name?

"You live very near the dragon, Perdoneg," she said.

Vijocka nodded. "The evidence of his destruction fills the northern sky," she said. "Many of the people of the village Rune-dar have left their homes and fled southward, for the drag-on often comes to rest on a hill near their village. More leave every day, for their terror sears their hearts and devours their courage more surely than the dragon might do their flesh. I have spent many weeks now in prayers and fasting for the words of the spell that might protect the people. The words do not come. There is no magic to stay this fell creature—its magic is too great for those of our order."

She said it with such quiet courage that Marwen knew it was true.

"It is strange then that the dragon does not use his magic but only his fire."

Marwen stopped, her bowl of tea halfway to her mouth. Her

reflection in the bowl was gold-skinned and lambent, astonished. It was true, but it had not occurred to her.

"He kills like a beast," Vijocka continued, "with talon and tail, and with fire. But he uses no magic. His fire is weapon enough, though. He seeks the wizard and believes that the wizard and his heir, if he has one, will come to do battle with him if he continues to kill. But it is more than that. It is vengeance upon Morda-hon, that great wizard of ancient days, for keeping him in his prison for many ages. It is sickness and hatred. It is darkness and evil." Her head and neck were very erect as she spoke, and her eyes were lit with a quiet flame. "We will be without hope when the dragon uses his magic."

The wind blew on Marwen's tea, ruffling her reflection. She looked up. "There is one who is seeking a way to rid us of this evil," Marwen said. "It is to him that I go, for I would help him."

"You mean Prince Camlach," Vijocka said. "He stayed with me on his journey northward, while his men slept in my fields. How do you, a Venutian, know the Prince?"

"I helped him once," Marwen said. She warmed her hands around her bowl, swirled the muddy leaves at the bottom. "He asked me to help him stop Perdoneg, but I refused."

"And now you have come to help," Vijocka said. She shook her head. "You are brave, for had I lost my tapestry, I would not face death willingly until I had it again. Do you know what is in it?"

Marwen shook her head. "I have never seen it."

Vijocka looked at her long and hard, and Marwen met her gaze.

"You do realize what would happen to you if you were to die before your tapestry were fulfilled?"

Marwen smoothed her skirt with her hands. "If I die without my tapestry, I know I must go to the land of the lost and labor in Perdoneg's kingdom. Yes, I am afraid, but I am more afraid to run away."

The dark woman leaned over and plucked a dead leaf from a stalk of leaflullen. Grondil's hands on Vijocka's arms, Marwen thought, strong and rough, steady as stone, and she thought then that she could utterly trust this Oldwife.

"Vijocka, on my way to the Oldest, the One Mother sent me a seeing. In it the dragon called me 'daughter of Nimroth, heir to the wizard.'" The dead leaf in Vijocka's hand crumbled to dust. "I think it might be me that the dragon seeks, for the wizard himself no longer dwells among mortals."

Vijocka rubbed the leafdust in her hands, back and forth, again and again, until it was gone. She closed her eyes, held her hands to her face, and breathed deeply.

Finally she said, "Prince Camlach told me that he thought he had found the wizard's heir. I remember well his words, his hope."

"I have no tapestry to prove such a thing," Marwen said.

Vijocka looked at her but with the eyes of one who is seeing the past. Her hands rested still and spellwise on her knees. "The house of Nimroth, the poet, is not many miles north of here," she said. "When I was growing and serving my apprenticeship, he would come of a year and sing and tell his tales and then be gone again for many suns. As a girl I remembered his visits with joy, for they were holidays, and the work would be put aside to listen and dance to his music, even by my mother, the Oldwife.

"One day I became ill, so ill that even my mother could not cure me. She had not always treated her calling with respect, but she loved me and searched the lore books day and night for a spell that would abate the fever that burned my life-fires lower each day. Finally I became delirious. I remember that, as my mother cast herself across my bed, weeping, a woman appeared inside the room. Old she was, wrinkled and crippled with years. Her shoes were the yellow of the sun, and her apron shone with the blue of heaven. She beckoned to me, and I longed to go to her. And then something happened: Nimroth, the poet, appeared in the open door of our house, only his face was not smiling and innocent as I remembered it from days past but sad and full of wisdom, and in his hand was a staff that glowed with a radiant white light. Gently, lovingly, he put his hand round the old woman's shoulders and led her out of the house.

"Thereafter I returned to good health. My mother had been asleep with sorrow when all this happened, and so I carried my secret alone, letting it ripen inside me, leading me deeper into the magic. Nimroth did not speak to me of it when he came to the village as a poet, though sometimes he caught me looking at him. Then he would stop smiling, and the wisdom in his eyes would shine.

"One day he came through our village and to my window. He was going away, he told me, for a long time, perhaps forever. I offered to provide him with an heir (though shyly and clumsily), but he merely smiled and seemed glad to know that I had not forgotten or thought it was delirium that day when I discovered he was the wizard. He told me that the dragon Perdoneg was growing in power, that one day he would escape his prison and come seeking to kill the wizard and his heir. He told me that if the wizard and the heir were killed, there would be no peace, neither in this life nor the next. He explained that what he was about to do would thwart the dragon. Then he would speak no more of it. I fed him and he left."

Vijocka drained her bowl.

"But now, my friend, if you would so honor me, I will share your sadness. Tell me how you come to be without your tapestry, and if I have any magic to help you, I will."

Marwen spoke haltingly of how her mother, Grondil, had hidden her tapestry so that the people would not offer her, a nameless orphan, as a gift to the Taker. She did not weep when she told Vijocka of her life as a soulless one, but she wept as she told of her joy when she discovered that she did have a tapestry.

"But it was destroyed," Marwen said glancing toward her apron pocket.

"Was there no witness to your tapestry?" Vijocka asked.

"None at my birth and only one after." She drew Cudgham-ip carefully out of her apron pocket and placed him on the ground. He yawned and blinked his bleary eyes and slowly began moving about the room, devouring insects that hid among the wild flowers. Marwen followed him with her eyes. "This is my stepfather, Cudgham. He showed me where my tapestry was hidden, and before I could see it, he thrust it in the fire. In my rage I cast a spell on him that did this. Later I tried to reverse the spell, but I could not."

Vijocka watched the ip crawl about the room, his legs heavy and slow, his tongue quick.

"To reverse the spell, you must forgive him," Vijocka said at last.

Marwen stared. She felt the heat rising in her face.

"Then he must remain always an ip," she said slowly.

"Time is not your friend," Vijocka said. "If you truly mean to do battle with Camlach against Perdoneg, likely you will die."

"Yet I cannot forgive. Because of what he has done, I am doomed to live in torment."

"We give ourselves up to torment, Marwen," Vijocka said. "You cannot have forgotten that. If the spell is reversed, he can stand witness while I make you a new tapestry."

Then Marwen was angry and her voice was sharp.

"What if he refuses? He burned it once, he may have some reason for not wanting me to have a tapestry. What if he lies, if he witnesses wrongly?"

"He tells me nothing," Vijocka said calmly. "By way of a spell, I can know his mind concerning the tapestry. If he does not cooperate, return him to his ip form if you wish."

The wind blew through the east window and carried the word *wish* off to be dropped on some soul far away.

Know his mind? Marwen had never heard of such a spell. To know the mind of another would certainly be great magic. She caught herself gaping and closed her mouth with a snap.

"Give me this spell," she said.

"It is for all to know," Vijocka said easily, gesturing toward her collection of lore books. "It is in the *Songs of the One Mother*, and its success depends only on the wielder of the words."

Restraining her greed to know, Marwen calmly opened the pages of the ancient book. It was almost the same as her own, lacking only the pictures of dragons that had been drawn in the margins. "I will see my tapestry in Cudgham's mind myself," Marwen said. Vijocka's finger stretched in one long plane to point out the passage. Marwen read and read again. She closed the book and said the words aloud.

She looked up and saw herself reflected in Vijocka's dark eyes. The fear that suddenly sped through her veins like cold spring-water did not show, did not radiate from her like dark wings. Then she realized that it was not fear that coursed through her body after all but magic. Her bowels burned with an ice-born heat, and her mind filled with windsong. She felt the earth spinning beneath her, alive, not beastlike but womanlike. A whole and beautiful being whose tapestry was the sky and whose spirit blew like wind and cloud over its body of mountains and swelling ocean. And she knew that it spun for her and for all the children of the earth. She touched the mind of the One Mother and worshipped her.

Marwen reeled and felt Vijocka's cool strong hands helping her to lay on the greatrug.

"Your mind is the tool," Vijocka whispered in her ear. "You must use it, focus your thoughts. If you let your thoughts run free, you will not succeed. Think of the mind of the ip, of your stepfather. But be sure you are strong."

Marwen reached out tendrils of thought toward the green and rust-striped lizard that crept on the floor beside her. Her vision clouded, as if breeze-blown mists were before her eyes. She felt her legs grow heavy, as though she herself were in the form of an ip, and she felt her tongue flick out as quickly as a flame leaping, felt herself floating as sparks and cinders on the wind.

Something was wrong. There was a tearing noise behind her eyes, and the sound of wind in her throat. She knew she was no longer in the mind of the ip. A deeper wish had transported her to a mind more powerful, a mind of darkness and misery, a mind bubbling with hot black magic.

When next she could see again, it was through the eyes of the dragon.

Perdoneg was unaware that he had been violated, Marwen knew. Marwen had come into the heart of the dragon's psyche, and there, all around her like a raging storm, screamed the words, "My tapestry ..."

She was in the dragon's mindbeing, its thoughts whipping

and blowing like grass before the wind, like sand in a windstorm, and hate and fear squalled together in a tempest of emotion. Always at the center, like the eye of the hurricane, were the words, "My tapestry ... my tapestry ..."

Through the dragon's eyes, she could see a hill and on the slope of the hill, a shack around which flowers bloomed in a mist of color. Flowers poured over the edge of the windowboxes, and even the roof was a cloud of petal, leaf, and swaying stems. It was the shack she had seen in the vision spring. But the eyes of the dragon did not see the shack and the flowers, only the slim shape of a man, a young man it seemed, dressed in a green tunic and fine brown boots who was stealthily crawling up the slope.

Marwen knew that the young man was Prince Camlach.

The dragon was going to kill him, of that there was no doubt. Unless she could distract him for a moment.

"Perdoneg," she said with her mind.

Shock. Astonishment. Then glee. She felt the dragon's eyes turn inward, away from the climbing figure on the slope, and the window through which she had come shut tight.

Above the din, quiet but piercing, came the dragon's voice.

"Marwen."

It was caressing, even lustful, and Marwen thrilled unwillingly to the sound of it.

"Marwen, child of power, you have come to me," the voice rang. "You are mine."

"No!"

"I have seen your tapestry in the lands of the dead, its spirit, its shadow, lost in a place where only the Taker could find it." The dragon laughed, and his laughter echoed as if in a canyon.

Marwen felt herself shut in, trapped. Camlach would be safe now, but there was no way out for her.

Marwen cried, "You are evil!"

"What is evil? Do you not think evil has its own reward, as does good? That is the only choice you have—to choose your reward. Ask learning of me." The voice was calm and utterly, utterly sane.

"Pity the dark and the untruth," Marwen murmured, repeating aloud from the *Tenets of the Tapestry.*

"Pity it not," said the dragon. "It simply is. Without darkness and lies there could be no light and truth. I need not kill you, Marwen. I can take you alive to reign as queen of my kingdom. Only tell me where your father is."

Marwen tried not to hear. His voice was seductive and beautiful. Behind it she could hear the storm raging on.

"Let me go!" Marwen shouted in a disembodied voice. The words were lost in the din of psychic noise around her, and Marwen was terrified. The spell included no words for protection from a mind stronger than one's own. Her body lay in a death-like trance while her mindforce faced an eternity of entrapment in the haunted mind of the dragon.

She thought of spells of freeing, loosening, revealing, until briefly she remembered the hands of Vijocka, steady and magic-wise, and Marwen became still.

"Be calm," she told herself. She remembered Vijocka's counsel to focus her thoughts and be strong. In that moment she realized that the dragon could not hear the storm of his subconscious, did not know that she could hear it.

"I am the wizard's heir," Marwen whispered, and the words echoed in a hiss above the clamor. She felt power stretch from her like unfolding wings.

"I am the wizard's heir," she repeated. "Perdoneg, why do you not use your magic? Where is your tapestry?" Her voice rang softly like a musical note in a storm. The dragon did not answer, but the noise increased.

"You will free me, for only I can find your tapestry. It is my right, my gift...."

Though her voice was still and small, she knew the dragon heard. She waited.

When the window of the dragon's mind opened, she flew away.

Marwen could hear, feel, smell for many winds before she could see or speak. She heard the soft steady chanting of Vijocka in trance and the plea of freshwind through the east window; she felt the warmth of the noonmonth sun on the left side of her body and the rough woven texture of the greatrug beneath her; she smelled the burning incense of Vijocka's spellworking and new-blooming sweesle.

It was windeven when, emerging from the haze of her semi-consciousness, Marwen could see the form of Vijocka, cross-legged and hunched.

"It was you," Marwen said, her voice croaking, her lips dry and sticky. "It was you that gave me wings...."

Vijocka's chanting stopped abruptly when Marwen spoke. She slowly opened her eyes, but she did not move or speak for a long moment.

Finally she said, "No, Marwen. It was by your own power that you have done what you have done. I kept your body alive while you did it. Never have I seen such power. Not even the wizard Farrell of old could have done such a thing."

"Where is my ip?" Marwen asked, not hearing.

"You—you were with Perdoneg...." Vijocka said softly, her eyes fixed and staring at the tray of smoking incense. Marwen nodded.

Vijocka opened her mouth as if to speak. Then in a fluid movement, she bent on one knee before Marwen and rose again.

"I honor the heir," she said simply. "None other than the wizard could enter the mind of the dragon and return to tell of it."

Marwen reached out to Vijocka. For a time they grasped each other's forearms, quiet, desperate. Marwen laughed a brief breathless laugh, and Vijocka laughed, too, almost a gasp or a sob.

Finally Vijocka said, "What will you do?"

"I must go. He is seeking me. He will know now that I am close—hopefully, he will have no idea how close. His tapestry is the key," Marwen said sitting up groggily. "I believe it is at my father's house. Perhaps when I see the tapestry, I will know what to do."

Vijocka watched her with unseeing eyes. "Yes, the lore books tell of Morda-hon hiding the dragon's tapestry. I remember now. It is a little-known detail. Nimroth must have found it. But surely this dragon, who has lived century upon century and has memory of the beginnings and endings of kings and rivers, would remember what was in his own tapestry."

"He remembers," Marwen said. "His desperation has to do with its finding and its fulfilling, but I was not strong enough and did not penetrate deeply enough to know any more than this for certain."

Still Vijocka had not moved, and Marwen noticed how sallow her brown skin had become, and her lips and fingernails were a dusky purple. Marwen felt dizzy when she got on her feet, but thirst drove her, and then she held out a cup of water for Vijocka.

The woman drank quickly, sloppily. Marwen put an arm around her to steady her.

"How long have you been like this?" Marwen asked stroking her black silky braid.

"You have been in trance for one windcycle," Vijocka said. Cudgham-ip crawled into Marwen's lap. Marwen sat very still. She put out one finger and stroked his leathery back.

"Cudgham-ip, the time has come to return you to your proper form," she said. "Before I lived in Perdoneg's mind, I touched the mind of the Mother. And I worshipped her. I worship her, Cudgham, the One who gives me my magic, who loves me ... and you." Marwen closed her eyes and pursed her lips together. She opened them again. "For her I do forgive and free my heart to reverse the spell. Perhaps then you will help me regain my tapestry."

The huge helmeted head of a man appeared in the east window. He was bearded and sweating. "Oldwife of Rute, let your hands be blessed!" he bellowed.

Marwen and Cudgham-ip both jumped.

The man's eyes touched Marwen and then rested on the ip that was running as quickly as it could across the dirt floor.

In less than two breaths, the soldier fit his bow and shot the ip, pinning it to the floor. It squirmed for a short time and died.

CHAPTER FIFTEEN

BELIEF THAT DWELLS IN THE HEAD IS LESS
WORTHY THAN BELIEF THAT DWELLS IN THE
HANDS AND THE FEET AND THE BACKBONE OF
MAN. —*TENETS OF THE TAPESTRY*

"I AM SORRY," the man was saying to Vijocka. "How was I to know the lass had an ip for her familiar?"

Vijocka was not paying any attention to him. Her arms were around Marwen, consoling her. Marwen was not aware of sadness. Inside her was a horrible darkness, but she could not name it sadness. Having Vijocka's arms around her felt good, and she ached for Grondil's touch and longed to be with her.

"I said I was sorry and that is a better apology than more deserving ones have received. Now, Oldwife of Rute, the Prince sends for you, for he has need of your magic."

Marwen looked up.

"Camlach?"

The soldier named Torbil glared at her with black eyes. "I like not the sound of his name in your mouth, Venutian wench."

Vijocka began to protest, but Marwen stopped her with a gesture.

"I am Marwen Oldwife. I will go with you in place of Vijocka."

"I go with no Venutian witch."

"Silence!" Vijocka said. "If Camlach is in need of magic, her's is the greater."

"Nevertheless ..."

"I will not go," Vijocka said. "My own people need me. Take Marwen or take no one."

The soldier cursed into his beard and turned away from the window to wait for Marwen impatiently.

"Go quickly," Vijocka said. "I will do the rights for Cudgham-ip."

Marwen nodded but did not move.

"Is there no hope now, Vijocka? Can I never have my tapestry?"

Vijocka paused before she answered. "I know of no way, but perhaps you will find one. You are the wizard's heir."

Marwen stood unmoving until Vijocka pushed her gently out the door. "Hurry," she said, her voice hushed, urgent. She walked with her to the wingwand fields where the soldier waited.

Cullerwind wailed in the hollows and blew Marwen off balance. The dark clouds in the north had dispersed.

"Take fresh beasts and leave your own here to rest," Vijocka said.

She introduced Marwen to a sleek young beast, grass-green with black wing markings. "This is Fallspar, and this is Grafewing," she said giving the soldier a heavy-set male with mottled blue and gray wings.

She took Marwen aside just before she mounted.

"Take care. You hold a prince's heart in your hands if I am not amiss, and that is a great power in itself." Marwen remembered Camlach climbing up the hill, foolishly, bravely before the dragon's eyes, and she thought what a great thing it would be to hold that good heart as her own.

"Truly, Vijocka?" She wondered why this belief came harder to her than any other now.

The Oldwife nodded. Torbil grunted impatiently. Marwen waved and signaled the wingwand to fly.

"Go with the blessings of the Mother!" Vijocka called as they rose into the air.

The green wings of Fallspar met at the top, enfolding Marwen in an envelope through which the noonsun shone, then dropped until they met at the bottom revealing to her a panoramic view of the land that changed with almost every other wingbeat.

Fleshy pale-leafed weeds, almost as high as her waist, grew profusely on the foothills far below. They were the largest vegetation Marwen had ever seen, and she wondered at the sight.

Her wonder soon faded, however, when, after traveling through nuwind, they rounded a low soft-sloped mountain and came in sight of true mountains. With each wingbeat they loomed larger, and Marwen had to remind herself to breathe. Depthless and hazy they seemed from this distance, layered shades of lavender, flat and sharp-edged. Below them was a hill unremarkable by comparison.

When they landed on the lower reaches of the hill, Marwen discovered she had underestimated the size of the pale plants. Their tender green fingers reached almost to the height of her breast. Yellow blooms like rings of jewels adorned the tallest. She felt as small as a hearthcat hiding in the grasses.

"What is this plant?" Marwen asked as the soldier placed socks on the wingwands' antennae.

"Fedderweed," he said gruffly. "It is poisonous. It seems to be good only to provide cover."

The wingwands ignored the fedderweed and grazed on the grass that lay crushed and blown beneath like old yellow hair.

"I have never seen such large flowers...." Marwen said.

"Silence!" the soldier growled, crouching in the weeds. He pointed to the hill that rose before them. "See there. That is Perdoneg's favorite sleeping place, around the top. He is gone now, but your voice is loud enough for a dragon's ears to hear all the way to the border."

The hill looked familiar to her and beautiful but for the blackened patches where the grass had been burned away.

"Where is Prince Camlach?"

The soldier nodded toward the hill.

"Near the top of that hill is a house that Perdoneg continues to spare." Marwen looked in the direction that Torbil gestured. Nestled in a dimple of the hill near the age-worn summit was the small house of clay and straw bricks, thatch-roofed and snug, just as she had seen it twice before. She could see only vaguely the wild flowers that grew over the fence, around the doorway of the house, and out of the coping stones, the delicate color of flowers that grow without seeding in wild places. But all around the yard, where flowers had been when Marwen had had the seeing in the well, was a black charred scar, and in soft dark lumps on the slope lay the roasted remains of the weedsheep that had once grazed there.

Torbil was whispering, a sound like rolling gravel. "He senses when anyone comes near it and kills all who approach. How the Prince got up there only the Mother knows. Crob has gone to bring some of the women and children from Rune-dar to the house, but before he left he sent me for the Oldwife of Rute.

His message to her was: 'There is some magic in this house. Come help us find it.' I am to go with you to the house."

Marwen could hear the fear in his voice. If she failed, he, too, would die.

But Marwen was not afraid. From the beginning of time, she had been meant to see this house, to go into it, and to find its secret—the power that preserved it from Perdoneg's fire. Still the gods did not love the foolish and would expect her to use good sense. She could not risk walking boldly up the side of the hill, for the wings of the dragon were swift and silent, and if he were not here now, he could be in the next breath.

Marwen knelt before a particularly large fedderweed, its branches reaching out like thin arms, its fleshy leaves finely veined.

"Hail, lady fedderweed, dressed in green lace and jeweled in gold. I am Marwen Oldwife of Marmawell, daughter of Nimroth, the wizard who once walked among you. I need your help."

Immediately the wind sang softly through the plant's leaves. Marwen listened, and it seemed after a time that she heard, beyond the fair song of the fedderweed, a deeper voice, a richer song. She began to walk toward the sound.

"Come," Marwen whispered to the soldier. He stood staring as she walked a few paces and then, bending low, he rushed to catch up.

"I do not hold with any Venutian sorcery," he said behind her.

She gestured to him for silence. The song was one of great beauty and sadness and pain. It became louder as they came closer to the hill. They circled it to its northern slope.

Marwen's thighs cramped, walking hunched as she was, but the song grew ever nearer and stronger. At last, when they were practically at the foot of the hill, Marwen saw the singer.

She had no name for what she saw, and she stared open-mouthed. It was not grass or flower but a god of soil and stem, nevertheless. Beside it she felt soft and young. The soldier looked at her and said, "Tree. It is called tree." Then he thought for a moment and added, "There are trees in the mountains, but this one comes from a place where there are many such giant plants, and the wingwands could fit into the palm of your hand. Or so the legend goes."

Its huge stem was covered in tough brown hide, and its limbs were muscular and tuberous. One of the large branches, a fraction of the tree itself, had been torn away, leaving an open white wound and the remaining branches cupping cold sky where once had been living green.

Marwen shook her head in disbelief and walked slowly toward the tree. It smelled clean like rain, sweet like the earth, and in its wind-frayed leaves, the breezes tossed and played. Among its leaves were white fruit bearing down the branches.

"By the gods—Perdoneg! He's back!" Torbil whispered fiercely, his voice just short of shrieking. Marwen glanced upward a moment to the north sky where the sun burned hot and bright on the scales of a great winged creature. Before it flew a frantic group of wingwands and riders. She looked again at the tree.

"Ah," she said softly, circling the tree and touching it gently with her fingers.

"Hide us," Torbil said desperately.

Behind the tree the hill rose sharply upward, and where the tree's feet were rooted in the earth was a small cave.

"We'll be burned alive," he said. "The dragon can smell human flesh a furlong away."

"There," Marwen said pointing to the cave. "This is the gift the tree gives."

She bent and hunched into the cave. It was cool and moist.

In only a few paces, Marwen was forced to go on hands and knees through a tunnell-like aperture that opened suddenly to a large womb of blackness. Somewhere off to her right, water fell and splashed her with points of cold.

The soldier had followed behind, his huge hot breaths on her heels, but he had stopped and now was lodged in the tunnel.

"My shoulders won't go through," he grunted.

"Hush," Marwen whispered. "This is a sacred place. If you cannot come in, you are not meant to be here. Stay and wait for me."

With a grunt he pushed his way through at last, leaving shreds of shirt and skin clinging to the rock.

Marwen held out her hands, palms together, and whispered an incantation. Slowly, between her palms, a cool white flame grew until, carefully, she pulled one hand away, and the flame nestled brightly in the other. It illuminated a stone stairway before them.

"Great Mother!" exclaimed the soldier, and Marwen knew from the tone of his voice it was a prayer and not a curse. The cave was a large vault of red granite that glittered from floor to ceiling in Marwen's bit of werelight, but more beautiful still was the waterfall shrouded in a soft mist.

Lying beside a rock basin filled with water was an old tapestry pouch.

"The house must be at the top of the stairs," said the soldier. "Come. Once in the house, we are safe."

"Wait," she said. She hunched down to look at it more closely. Embroidered into the pouch was a dragon without eyes, writhing in the wind.

"Great Gods! What are you doing? Come!" He grabbed her arm, but she wrenched it from his grasp without looking away from the pouch.

Her fingers jumped when she touched the pouch, alive as it was with magic. Carefully, the thin old threads grasped in her fingers, she pulled the top right corner of the tapestry out. A tree had been woven there, a tree with white fruit, and against the tree leaned a staff. Nimroth's tapestry, not Perdoneg's. So fragile were the threads that they began to tear beneath her gentle touch, and she tucked the tapestry back into the pouch.

It had been left here for her by her father. He had gone to his death without his tapestry so that she would find it, though she did not know why. Marwen felt herself growing heavier and lighter all at once. Her soul was sinking close to the earth, acquiring weight and substance, and at the same time becoming tiny as a wind-borne seed, thin as the wingscale of a wingwand.

"Come, there is no time," Marwen said quietly. She closed her fist on the werelight, snuffing it. They climbed the stone staircase in silent haste and in darkness, going straight up as if in a long narrow chimney. At last Marwen felt a bit of wind on her face and saw a patch of light above her, round and blue as a moon.

The man below her was becoming claustrophobic and swore at himself at close intervals, finally cursing Marwen as well.

"If Perdoneg hears you, one breath of his fire down this hole will roast us both," Marwen whispered. As if in testament, the moon of light above went out briefly, eclipsed by dragon-darkness.

"Can't breathe," he muttered, and then he was quiet.

The hole emerged into a grotto. She pulled aside a curtain of flowers and saw that they faced the east window of the little house. It was not far to the doorway of the house but far enough to die. The air of noonmonth felt thick and warm in her mouth after the cool thin air of the cave. With a brief prayer,

Marwen picked up a pebble from the floor of the cave, kissed it and tossed it through the window. The soldier entered the grotto then, sweating and bloody, filling almost the entire space with his body. It was he that Camlach saw when he peered out the window, and he to whom the Prince gestured.

"Great gods, the dragon is above us!" Torbil half-whispered, half-shrieked.

"Do as I say," Marwen said.

The soldier nodded, gripping his sword hilt convulsively.

"Hold this tapestry pouch with me, and when I say, run."

She pictured the blind dragon in the wind, the blind dragon of the tapestry pouch. She whispered her strongest spell of hiding and slipped through the curtain of flowers. "Run!"

Like phantoms they darted around the corner and into the door.

A roar like a winter wind filled their ears, and the straw-chinked bricks around the doorway glowed with flames. A figure was beating out the glowing straw with his cloak. Torbil joined him, but Marwen stood still, feeling the power in the house like a heavy quiet as her eyes adjusted to the dimness. Soon there was the smell of smoke and baked mud but no more flames. Perdoneg would not or could not destroy the house.

The two men stood panting, their faces streaked black and their hair gray with ash and soot, before Camlach finally looked at Marwen.

The Prince appeared years older than when Marwen first looked at him, but as recognition dawned on his face, the extra years melted away.

"Marwen!" he exclaimed.

He strode forward as if he would take her in his arms, and then he stopped, and his smile faded. Marwen faced him calmly, soberly. He was tanned, and his eyes shone with health. His broken nose had set a little oddly, but it seemed only to make his face more manly.

"I was coming to you when your man found me at Rute," she said. There was nothing soft in her voice.

"I trust he has treated you like a princess."

Marwen glanced at Torbil, who stood whey-faced and agape, and said, "Most royally. But we are thirsty. Have you anything to drink?"

Camlach shook his head. "Nothing. And no food. There is nothing here, nothing of value at all that I can find. Perhaps this is not Nimroth's house after all."

She held out to him the worn threadbare tapestry pouch she had found. "This is his house. I found this hidden in the cave beneath the hill. It is not Perdoneg's tapestry but Nimroth's. It will help us, for I know the story it tells. Now we need only the dragon's tapestry...."

She began to search the house with her eyes and then with her magic.

It consisted of a main room, a smaller room and a pantry, all unlit by anything save the east window.

Camlach cleared his throat. "But where is Maug?"

"I left him behind," Marwen said, looking in every corner. She glanced at Camlach. "No, do not smile, Prince Camlach, for I have possibly left him to his death. I left him alone in the hills not a quarter the way to Loobhan."

"Did he give you my gift?"

"Gift? He gave me nothing," Marwen answered.

"I knew you would not take it—the magical blanket that Crob and Politha gave to me—and so I told Maug to give it to you when we were apart."

Marwen smiled wryly. "Now I need not worry. Maug will be all right."

In the main room was only a greatrug, once of much richness, now gray with dust and stained with bird droppings. There was a clay table decorated with elaborately printed runes and varnished to a high gloss. On the table was an hourglass. Above the fireplace, where some birds had made a rough nest, was a row of pots, once shiny and now covered in a layer of dust. In the smaller room was a hammock cradling a layer of dry leaves, and everywhere were books piled in dusty stacks. The pantry had little in it but a broom hosting a colony of thinwings, a net of bulbs hanging, and strings of herbs dried paper thin.

"Have you tried digging in the floor?" she asked. She kept her voice quick and strong. She was aware of him near her.

"The wizard laid a brick floor," Camlach answered. "Marwen, I'm glad you've come."

Marwen ran her hands over the scorched walls, pressing lightly against the warm brick, touching, pressing, until the pantry was the only room left.

"But a day's journey out of Kebblewok, I had a seeing," she said examining a crack in the pantry wall. There was nothing in it but a family of mudfleas. She could feel Camlach listening to her silence, waiting. "The dragon called me by name, called me Nimroth's daughter, heir to the wizard."

She reached up to touch the dried leaves hanging fragile and fragrant, but when she touched them, they turned to dust and sifted down, burning her eyes and choking her.

"I knew it," he said.

"Did you?"

A coldness filled Marwen's soul. She was not the same little girl who had cried when people hated her. In those days the people told her about herself, as a mirror did. They had defined her, had given her size and form, had erased her with one word: *soulless*. But now, though she had no tapestry, no one could take her soul away from her nor the reality that she was the white wingwand and the wizard's heir, the Mother's child. Even now, scar tissue was forming on old wounds, and in place of pain would be strength and toughness.

In the hourglass, rimmed with gold about the top and bottom, the peak of silver sand was still, as though all time had frozen and was awaiting a mortal hand to move it. Marwen lifted it and turned it bottom up. The sand did not flow but remained a mass in the top of the glass, solidified by the years. Slowly she turned toward him.

"Look at me, Camlach," she said, clutching the hourglass against her stomach. "Look into my eyes and tell me that I am soulless."

He looked, but she knew he saw no reflection of himself. For she had absorbed him with her eyes, drunk him deep into the ash-gray of her eyes, brought him in and given him back, only full-sized and beautiful, as she saw him.

"Marwen ..."

She turned away. "I hid the dragon's tapestry so well with my spells that even I cannot find it," she said.

Just then the side of the house shook with the blow of an arrow. Camlach's head snapped toward the east window.

"Crob is back," Camlach said, striding to the east window. "That is his signal for help."

"Crob?" Marwen ran to Camlach's side. "He is trapped on the hillside?"

"The dragon torments the city of Rune-dar when he is not flying in the south inner lands. He thinks the people there must know something of the wizard. I asked Crob to bring the sick and young from there to this house, thinking they would be safe here." Camlach's face was pale. "My brother is coming southward from Duma with fresh fighting men and stronger weapons. I had hoped he would be here by now."

They watched as the dragon's shadow circled around them, rippling black over the slope. At the foot of the hill, Crob and the small group of villagers crouched.

The dragon blocked the sun like a black cloud, and Marwen saw it for the first time with her mortal eyes. She was mesmerized. Its wings were like veined sails on huge bones, full of bloody magic. Its neck arched in a dark ageless pride, and from its mouth it vomited a bright hot wind.

Camlach unsheathed his sword.

"What are you doing?" Marwen asked.

"Crob will die and the people with him. He was following my orders." Marwen watched aghast as Camlach stood in the doorway taking several deep breaths and then ran with all his strength down the hill, shouting challenges and insults to the dragon as he went. Torbil cursed and followed at his heels. Perdoneg laughed, and a star of fire blazed from his mouth. The wind throbbed drumlike beneath the beast's immense wings, and on the ground below, Marwen could see the dragon's thin black shadow darken the faces of the villagers. There was a gleam of arrows in the sun, needlelike against the dark scaly hide of the dragon's belly. Marwen stopped breathing as she saw the creature descend, roaring his anger and filling the sky with an ash-flaked heat. One man fell, engulfed in flames, twisting and writhing silently in fire. All around him the villagers screamed. Clutching their faces, falling on their children, they let the man die, the man Marwen knew was Crob.

She ran from the house on to the crest of the hill.

"Perdoneg!" she cried. "I am Marwen, daughter of Nimroth. I have come." Though her voice could not have carried, the dragon hovered, spun about and bucked, and began to fly toward her, forgetting his play with the terrified villagers and with Camlach.

Marwen ran back into the house, stood in the center of the room and clamped a hand over her mouth, quelling her nausea, swallowing her screams. Perdoneg's tapestry was here. She could feel its potent magic. But she had covered it too well with her own spells, spells on top of Nimroth's spells, layers of magic like dust, like fine ash.

She threw her arms into the air and then bent them over her head as if to protect it from descending flames. She felt a cooling sweat on her forehead. From a great distance away, it seemed, Marwen heard the dragon's voice like wind in a canyon, "Come to me Marwen. You are mine."

She looked up, trying to breathe normally, feeling the magic flood through her soul like music, a heavy horrible music, a strain remembered from a nightmare. "I need to know where the tapestry of Perdoneg is," she whispered aloud into the deepening dimness of the house, for Perdoneg blocked the sun from the window. "What spell? What spell?"

But there was no answer, no spell, no answer. The greatrug was beneath her feet felt cool and silken, and her legs tingled weakly. Her head felt heavy on her neck. She sat on the rug, seeming to float gently down.

And so now all was lost. Perdoneg would take her to his kingdom of lost and unfinished souls, and then he would return and rule all of Ve. Sometimes light and truth prevailed, and sometimes in the ages of man, dark and untruth prevailed. Her name would go down forever in the songs that survived as the last of the wizards, the wizard who failed before the magic of Perdoneg. And she would live the long night of death with the vision of good gentle Crob burning to bones before her eyes. In that moment she almost wished she were soulless.

"I am waiting, Marwen, daughter of Nimroth," the dragon hissed with a voice like a hailstorm.

She groaned and lay on the greatrug, pressing her face into its dusty threads. Before her eyes, woven into the rug, was the image of a white wing.

She touched it. She brushed at it, pressed it with her hand.

She sat up quickly, her heart pressing against her breastbone. Wildly, roughly, she brushed the dust away and scraped with her fingernail at the hardened skin of bird droppings until a white wingwand appeared. More frantically she beat at the dust until it choked her. She could see some of the designs in the rug.

On her hands and knees, forgetting to breathe or speak, Marwen ran her hands over the rich pictures that some skilled hand had woven: the white wingwand circled in ice gozzys, the flower of death; the staff also circled in white ice gozzys; the symbols of the skull, bloodpetal and witchwafer.

She pushed the table aside. It toppled over.

"This is not a greatrug," she cried aloud to no one. "This is Perdoneg's tapestry!"

Perdoneg was waiting, hunkered on the hill, when she walked out the door of the shack. At the bottom of the hill, the wingwands, laden with frightened people, flew into the air like light soundless birds, fleeing. Camlach and Torbil were creeping up the hillside, and Marwen lifted her left hand to stop them. The heavy tapestry, draped over her shoulders, trailed behind her in the dust. In the dragon's shadow, the house shrank into twilight, and before his dark beauty, Marwen was a pale phantom. In her right hand, the hourglass gleamed with a dull silver light.

Perdoneg's yellow eyes met hers lustfully. He opened his mouth to speak, but before he could, his great tooth-filled jaw went slack.

Marwen's voice sounded small and weak in the face of the dragon, but she could not raise it. "Yes. You are not mistaken, Perdoneg. This is your tapestry."

His body quivered and a foul smoke began to seep from his nostrils and the corners of his mouth. Claws huge and curved slid in and out of their thick sheaths. His tongue shone like charcoal and lolled in a black mouth.

"So, it has not been destroyed," Perdoneg said. His neck and back rippled and arched in triumph, and within his belly Marwen could hear the bubble and belch of tar and smoke.

"You know your tapestry cannot be destroyed by anything save your own dragonfire," Marwen said, and she pulled the tapestry closer about her body.

"I can kill you still," he hissed. "I need not burn you. Long have I awaited this moment." The pupils in his deep yellow eyes spun black and hideous, and Marwen looked beneath them and into his hot mouth.

"It is my gift to interpret the tapestry, Perdoneg. Before you kill me, I will do this for you," she said in a still quiet voice. Perdoneg answered nothing.

"At your birth you were promised in your tapestry that you would kill a wizard and his heir, and rule over a new age in which the dragons would once again prevail. Failing this, you must continue to dwell in the prison to which Morda-hon sent you in ages past."

"I will not fail," the dragon hissed, and a thread of blue flame

licked close to Marwen. "I will kill you with claw and tail, and
then I will seek your cowardly father, and he, too, will die. Evil
must have its time and its place in the world or that which is
good dies, too." The scaly hide over his haunches trembled and
twitched in anticipation.

Marwen nodded slowly. "But your time is not now, Perdoneg. You have come in body and pursued me with fire, but
your magic you cannot use. Your tapestry is unfulfilled, and so
your magic remains trapped in the lost lands. Furthermore, your
tapestry will not be fulfilled."

She held up the hourglass so that the gold base faced the
dragon, mirroring his leering face full of aged yellow teeth. She
made a spell for seeing, a long-worded difficult spell that sapped
the magic from her as with a great sucking mouth. She could
taste the saltiness of her own sweat on her lips. Perdoneg's fires
burned quiet.

Slowly an image moved in the gold, vague at first, then more
clear, until, reflected in Perdoneg's huge black pupils that dilat-
ed and contracted unceasingly, she could see the image of a man
walking. His head was bent and bearded with days, and his feet
moved with a dogged painful plodding toward a land shrouded
in mists and twilight. The land of the dead. The man bore a
staff, and on the crook of the staff were runes spelling a name:
Nimroth.

"Seventeen years ago," Marwen whispered dryly, "Nimroth
left his house and traveled by foot across the empty hills until he
came to the town of Marmawell where lived a young and fair
maiden named Srill. She knew she bore the wizard's heir, but
her secret died with her. While the child was yet a babe in arms,
Nimroth crossed the border of the land he was seeking, the land
of death. He walked into that land with eyes open, knowing well

the way, as all wizards do." She dropped the hourglass suddenly, as if it had taken all her strength to hold it up to that point. She forced her spine to straighten.

"You will not kill Nimroth, Perdoneg, for he is already dead. Your tapestry remains unfulfilled. Go back to your prison."

There was a silence as before the crack of lightening and then a scream like wind in fire vibrated the ground beneath her feet. "A trick!" he screeched. "It is a trick." His head writhed backward, and in his chest Marwen could hear a roar like wind in a chimney. Fire vomited from his mouth with blinding brightness until the sky darkened with smoke, and Marwen coughed and cowered in the doorway.

"You know it is no trick, Perdoneg," Marwen cried. Her voice was trembling so that she scarcely recognized it. She swallowed hard. "But if you need further proof, I have it. See." Without thinking, with shaking fingers, she took the richly woven tapestry pouch off her shoulder. Out of it she drew Nimroth's tapestry, her father's tapestry, and laid it, narrow and old, upon the ground before the dragon. She stared at the wondrous beautiful tapestry, the tapestry that spoke of foiling evil and defeating dragons and of walking open-eyed into death. She did not look up. In a moment the colors of the tapestry dimmed, and the threads loosened and filmed over with dust. In another moment it began to darken and shrink.

"You know this is Nimroth's tapestry, don't you, dragon. See, see how it blackens and shrivels and dissolves to dust before your eyes, as Crob's body on the hill is black and shriveled and returns to dust. As Nimroth is dead, so has his tapestry passed away."

By the time she was finished speaking, only the lifethread remained among the dust, warped and wrinkled as a worm. She stood and lifted her arm high, standing almost on tiptoe. She was elated, stunned, shaking with her own power. "Go, dragon, back to your prison," she commanded in the language of creation, not knowing she knew the words. Perdoneg's body thrashed, and his tail thudded upon the ground again and again and again, until Marwen's teeth seemed to loosen in her jaw, and she shrank under the protection of his tapestry. Finally his violence eased, and he brought his head close to hers, a great head full of teeth and tongue and mucous-filled eyes and nostrils crusted with carbon. Marwen choked in the burning stench and shrank back.

"Yes, I, too, am ruled by the law of the tapestry," Perdoneg hissed, "but my magic is great and cannot wholly be ruled by either tapestry or wizard. Before I return to my prison, a spell I cast upon you unto death, one slow and sure so that you may see the Taker coming from afar, remembering that you have no tapestry. And when you come to me in my kingdom, your sufferings will not end."

In one wind-filled beat, Perdoneg lifted his weight on great wings and rose into the air.

In three wingbeats he was gone.

CHAPTER SIXTEEN

"COULD IT THEN BE POSSIBLE THAT THE TAKER
IS NOT A TAKER AT ALL BUT A BRINGER, AND A
GUIDE—A GUIDE TO AN EXISTENCE FOR WHICH
THIS LIFE IS BUT A PREPARATION AND A PROV-
ING?" —"DEBATE OF THE OLDWIVES" FROM
SONGS OF THE ONE MOTHER

MARWEN IMMEDIATELY began to weave a spell of strengthening on the hold of Perdoneg's prison. She had been in the dragon's mind once, and so she knew the way by which he had escaped. When she was finished her spellworking, Camlach led her into the wizard's house.

Soldiers and citizens flocked to the hill as word spread that Perdoneg had been vanquished, but Camlach would not allow them to see her. Only Torbil did he allow to kneel silently before her, professing his service and devotion in a gruff stammering voice.

Marwen was weak and dizzy, so much of her powers had she expended. But it was not only fatigue that filled her. She was mortally sick.

She lay in a pool of light that poured in the east window, and

Camlach sat beside her, giving her sips of water. His face was drawn and dark and his mouth grim.

"I mourn Crob," Marwen said.

Camlach didn't answer for a moment. Then, "He came home to die. He told me. I didn't believe him. I have learned about belief today. I have learned from you, Marwen."

Through the window, norwind blew cool and constant, silvered with floating ash. Camlach leaned down and kissed her, a sad, hard, and needful kiss that made dying impossible to understand. He gathered her up in his arms and crushed his face against her hair.

"I want to live," she said, suddenly angry. "I want to live." She felt a cold numbness in her hands and feet, and far away, above the sounds of the gathering crowds without, she could hear music. The Taker's music.

The door of the house burst open, and Camlach leaped to his feet.

"My orders were to allow no one to enter!"

It was Torbil with the dusky figure of the Oldwife of Rute at his side.

"Forgive me, Lord, but this woman has come. She is the only believer I know, and I thought perhaps she could help."

Vijocka did not wait for permission from the Prince but walked regally to Marwen's side. Without speaking she ran her hands lightly over Marwen's body, stopping briefly at her forehead, breasts, and abdomen.

"Get me fedderweed," she ordered, "and water, good water, from the spring in the bowels of the hill. And bring to me from the fruit of the tree."

Torbil stumbled through the doorway in his haste to obey the Oldwife, and Camlach fell back to give her room.

"Can you help me?" Marwen asked. Her throat was swelling,

and the numbness had reached into her shoulders and hips.

"The only reason you are still alive is because of the power that is in you," Vijocka said. "I have no spell that can aid you, but when magic fails, there is still skill." All this she said while her hands worked steadily on the building of a fire. She stopped for a moment, looked at Marwen and then bent her face closer. Her voice was so soft it was heard by only Marwen.

"An Oldwife dies with dignity, a wizard with greatness of soul. Thou art both. If my art and thy magic should fail, die thou likewise."

Marwen closed her eyes slowly and then opened them and, with every effort of her will, nodded once.

Vijocka tended the fire quietly, taming it until it was hot and even. When the cavewater boiled, she set to steeping the silver-green fedderweed. The steam of it filled the shack with an acrid earthy smell. Into the tea Vijocka sprinkled some juice from the white fruit in her hand. By the time she offered some of it to Marwen, the girl's lips had become numb, and the liquid dribbled down her chin as she drank. Vijocka took the rest of the bitter tea and flung it on the fire with a quick prayer. Then she began to hum and then to sing, as if remembering a lullaby from her youth.

Beneath Nimroth's tree
deep dwelling in the wilderness—
there will I drink with you.
there will be a thousand thousand steps
through the dry wasteland
but only the desert is the freeing of our souls
and the purifying of our purposes.
There does the fruit bear sharp thorns,
the fields bring forth sand and rock,
and the rocks bring forth water.

Over dust and stony shallows,
the arid sky fills mind and heart and soul,
and when you are perishing of thirst
you will find my fountains,
wherein grows Nimroth's tree,
and I, deep dwelling in the wilderness,
there to drink with you.

"I have done all I can," Vijocka said then. "The Taker decides now."

Camlach and Torbil seemed far away, though they only sat against the wall on the other side of the room. It was the Taker who filled Marwen's hearing and vision, for as Vijocka washed her face caressingly, the old crone shuffled through the door. The men obviously saw nothing, but when Vijocka bowed low and moved away, Camlach stood slowly. Marwen could hear his breathing coming quick and shallow, and the whisper of his sword as it was unsheathed. The fire smoked cold.

Marwen saw the Taker more clearly now than she had ever seen her before. Her slippered feet were yellow like sunbutter against the dirt floor, but now Marwen saw that they did not quite touch the ground as she hobbled along. Around her thin shoulders her green dress hung like a garment on two pegs.

Her hands, knots of knuckle and bone, appeared as though she carried something in them, grasped together before her as they were. Her apron was the blue of the noonmonth sky, and where she had knotted the apron strings at her waist, the bow hung down like a transparent wingwand in flight. Brown and crinkled in silent laughter was her face, and Marwen could see that her eyes were the color of the mist on sunrising. Always her head nodded in mindless agreement.

Marwen could not speak, for the illness had bound her

tongue, but she kept her eyes open and her thoughts serene. She could feel her spirit struggling to be free of a body that was dying.

The Taker approached with her clasped hands outstretched, in the manner of beseeching, and when she was close to Marwen, she stopped still. Her toothless gums opened and closed, but no words did she speak.

"This is strange," Vijocka said, and Marwen saw her come forward, close to the Taker's hands. "What message, Mother Taker?"

The Taker knelt painfully before the dying fire and put her hands into the ash. With her stiff hands she worked the gray ash and the thin threads of smoke that rose into the shadow of something familiar, the ghostly image of a woven picture, the spirit of a tapestry. Marwen's tapestry.

She knew it immediately, that it was her own, as one would know the reflection of one's own face in the water. She tried to cry out, but she had no voice, and her lips would not move.

Vijocka knelt before the Taker so that the tapestry was before her eyes, and she began to memorize each image that shifted like sunlight on water between the Taker's outstretched hands. Marwen could see blue and white moons in a black sky and fountains of flowers: humelodia, ice gozzys, and stempellows. In the center of her tapestry was a mountain, a high snow-veined pinnacle of rock like the mountains she had seen far to the north of Rune-dar. Beneath the mountain was a white wingwand in flight, a key, a tree with white fruit, and ... a crown. Running the length of the tapestry was a single thread, the lifethread, the color of a summersun sky. At the top, like a border, was the sign of the staff, the wizard's sign.

Softly murmuring to herself and outlining with her finger,

Vijocka went over each symbol once, twice, three times before the Taker slowly folded the image into nothingness and lamely doddered out the door.

Vijocka watched her leave and then, her voice breaking, said, "The Mother has decided, Marwen. You live."

From that moment on, Marwen gained feeling and strength quickly. Now the future was not a wilderness of fear but a road with a clear direction and landmarks along the way. True, at the end of the road would still be the Taker, but Marwen had seen her eyes, that they were not the color of a blood-drained evening but the color of the mists at sunrise. She would remember that. The next windcycle, Camlach called for a feast in Marwen's honor in the dry hills near Rune-dar, and she stood before the throng briefly as they cheered her. But the songs were irreverent and bawdy, and Marwen thought that though they were glad to have Perdoneg conquered, still they did not believe in the magic or revere the wizard. Nevertheless, the story of the dragon and Marwen spread quickly and was put to song and embellished until it became more than it had been in reality.

Vijocka set to work immediately to weave again Marwen's tapestry, and when Marwen saw it, narrow and stiff with new threads, and touched with her own hand the sign of the staff along the top, she wept like a child.

"No wonder Cudgham burned the tapestry—the sign of the staff as clear as day. He must have thought he was doing you a kindness," Vijocka said.

When she was strong enough, Marwen walked to the bottom of the hill and plucked a piece of the white fruit from the tree. The peel was translucent and smooth, holding the white rays of the summersun overhead, shining as if with an inner light like a tiny moon. She tasted. It was cool like milk or snow, sweet like sugar or cream, and the meat of it was like a burst of light in her mouth. She laughed and felt the juice run down her chin. She bit into the fruit again.

It seemed for a moment as if she dreamed awake, or perhaps she had a seeing, she could not be sure. She thought she saw Nimroth, her father, plucking of the fruit of the tree for the last time before he began his journey south, south to the ends of Ve and life, plodding on and on into the fields of pain and beyond that into the fields of fear, taking himself with eyes open into the land of the dead, an intruder by his art, so that he might foil the dragon once again by denying him the opportunity to fulfill the promise of his tapestry. But before Nimroth died, he had loved and left his heir.

The fruit strengthened her, and each day thereafter she made her way to the bottom of the hill and ate of its magical fruit.

All during the lavender skies of the eveningmonths, Marwen lived in her father's house. She tended the flowers and dusted the books and planted a tiny garden. The villagers in nearby Rune-dar cared for her well, each day bringing her meat and vegetables and grain, and when they looked in the east window of a morning, they would find her deep in the study of her father's books. For she had found that in return for obedience, the Mother gave freedom—freedom to use the magic, freedom to feel, to know, and to be. She had passed through the narrow neck of the hourglass and found another expanding world in the next chamber.

Camlach returned often. He and his men were traveling the countryside, helping the villagers to rebuild their homes and replant their crops, and many times he flew to be with her.

Since she had become well again, he was shy with her, but one day as they walked under a sky filled with lavender clouds, he tried to kiss her once again.

She placed a finger on his lips to stop him. "This is an intimacy I save for the father of my children and the companion of my old age," she said.

"But that is me," Camlach said, half-pleading, half-indignant.

"What convinces you of this?" she laughed and then, teasing, she added, "Should you not first consult your tapestry?"

Camlach heard the teasing and grinned, but his eyes were shrewd and arrogant. "Yes," he said. "Perhaps I should."

"Without taking his eyes from Marwen's, he opened the pouch on his belt and extracted from it a narrow silken tapestry. He held it up before his face so that only the back threads, hinting at the majesty of design, were visible to Marwen's eyes.

In a moment his eyes peered over the top of the tapestry.

"I was right!" he said. "It says here, 'Do just exactly as you wish, Camlach.'"

Marwen frowned.

"Nonsense," she said. "It is sacrilege to make light of the tapestry, Prince or no."

"Perhaps, as an Oldwife," he said, holding it out, "you would do me the honor of interpreting my tapestry for me."

She sat on the grass and placed it on her lap, smoothing it, touching its silken threads, tracing its weft-faced patterns with her finger. It was opulent in design, a strong dense weave replete with symbols of power and justice, and washed in many blues. She said a spell for understanding and vision. The designs began to unfold in meaning before her eyes.

"So, shall I be a hero?" he asked sitting beside her.

She did not look at him. "A hero is not shown in his tapestry," she said mildly. "A hero's character is quietly woven from the threads of a hundred honest actions, a thousand selfless deeds."

He was silent. She felt him looking at her steadily.

She told Camlach of his heritage and the prophecies of his forefathers concerning his royal line; she told him of his strengths and talents and weaknesses. She showed him the dragonthread and the lifethread and told him that one day he would lead his people in war against a people who built great ships.

Her words flowed like song, without hesitation, with music. The magic was all around her like a charge in the air—her very hair felt alive, as though it could sense touch. And when Camlach spoke again, it seemed an irreverent intrusion on her trance.

"What, lady, means this white wingwand?"

She turned her eyes to the tiny white wingwand woven in a place of prominence. It was exactly like the soap carving he had given her. She had not seen it until now, and she puzzled over it for a time. It did not reveal itself to her, and she spoke a stronger spell for understanding.

Marwen saw the soap carving wingwand nesting in her tapestry pouch, and then Opalwing, still and white and beautiful in death. Then the vision was torn from her painfully. She knew what the white wingwand symbolized.

"It is my sign," she whispered. She looked up. He was grinning at her.

She handed him his tapestry. "You knew," she said, not smiling. She stood up. "The tapestry speaks an uncertain language at times." She made to walk away.

Camlach grabbed her arm, stopping her.

"I am not free to love," she said. It took no courage to say it. There was nothing else to be said. "I must judge Cudgham's tapestry and bury him in his own land. I must sing the Death Song for the people of my village. I must be witness for Maug at his tapestry making. Besides," and she hesitated, "you are the son of the king, Prince Camlach, and I am a Venutian exile."

The scars on his face that he still bore from his torture in Kebblewok stood out starkly on his pale skin. "You are the wizard," he said.

"I am the wizard's heir, yet to receive her staff, who still walks in the judgement of her home village. To the people of Marmawell, I was thrice a murderer. Before I can earn my staff, before I can love a prince," and she looked up into his eyes, "I must vindicate myself. And I must study, Camlach. I carry a great responsibility now for the people of Ve."

"I will go with you to bury Cudgham in Marmawell," Camlach said.

She shook her head. "When you are near me, I forget the world, for you become my world. I forget the pain of others in my joy. And then there are still my little demons of doubt. Why is it that when you say I am pretty, there is still distrust in my heart, and when you say you love, I must struggle to believe? I am not finished my task, Camlach, not yet."

He did not answer but took her hands in his and kissed the palms of them until her knees grew weak, and she begged him to leave her. He did leave straightway and did not say goodbye.

Days later, when she had made all preparations for her journey to Marmawell, two wingwands landed nearby, one roped to the other, and a rider approached that Marwen knew to be Torbil when he came closer.

He bowed briefly and said in his gravelly voice, "I am under orders to accompany you, Lady Marwen, to wherever your journey takes you and to continue as your guard until the Prince, in person, relieves me of my duties."

Under his black beard and moustache, she could see his dark skin flush. "Prince Camlach sends you this gift," and he gestured toward one of the wingwands. Only then did Marwen notice that it was pure white, with eyes like bloodred jewels. She laughed, a choked little sound at first.

"Is this some kind of punishment for you, poor Torbil, to guard a Venutian wench and on Venutian soil? What have you done to displease the Prince?"

There was a fierce pride in his eyes.

"No lady, this is a reward and an honor that I sought from the day that I pledged you my fealty."

"Thank you," Marwen said quietly. "I will need you."

THAT DAY at windeven, they began their flight west and south to the enchanted hills of Marmawell where once one could sit in the arms of the earth and smell the spice gardens on the estwind. Marwen felt completely and utterly free, high in the deep evening sky.

They would arrive on the eve of winterdark, when the Stumble would be high and quick, when only Opo nested on the horizon, and Marwen would remember the huts aglow with hearthfire. Then she would sing of her love for Grondil and Crob and Camlach, and for the Magic. It was the first thing she would do.

Printed in Canada